Dancing With Danger

Danger Incorporated

Book Ten

BY

OLIVIA JAYMES

www.OliviaJaymes.com

Chapter One

NOAH ANDERSON DIDN'T spend many evenings out on the town. He was far too busy running the Anderson ranch and all that entailed, plus he wasn't getting any younger. He couldn't party like he used to and then wake up before dawn to work all day. He needed – and liked – his sleep. A quiet evening at home with a cold beer and a good movie was far superior to loud music and a crush of people.

Duty called, however, and that's why he was sitting in a dimly lit hotel bar in Chicago. He'd been locked up with business partners and they'd capped today's meetings with a few cocktails and a handshake. Signatures on the dotted line would come later, but a deal that would make both sides a hell of a lot of money was incredibly close. He had one more meeting in the late morning and then he could go home.

The bartender nodded toward Noah's empty beer glass. "Another?"

Did he want another? He'd only planned on having one and then going back to his room, ordering some room service and making it an early night, but the urge to go back to his empty room wasn't strong.

"Sure. Thanks."

It wouldn't hurt to have a second. He could sit here at the bar, watch one of the televisions showing a football game, and maybe do a little people watching as well. It was a past-time that he enjoyed immensely, although he usually reserved it for the airport. A hotel bar would be just as good, though. Unlike in his hometown of Tremont where he knew everyone and they all knew him; here he was completely surrounded by strangers. He'd never see any of them ever again.

The bartender slid another draft in front of Noah. "Here on business?"

The guy was probably trained to make small talk with the customers. It was a safe question considering Noah was in a suit and this hotel was chock full of businesspeople.

"I am. It's been a good trip so far. I go home tomorrow."

"Where's home?"

"Tremont, Montana," Noah replied with a grin. "Don't worry if you haven't heard of it. No one has. It's a small town, too small to be on a map."

"Born and raised here in Chicago," the bartender said, wiping down a glass. "But I like the idea of a small town. It always sounds so friendly."

"It usually is but there are downsides. Everyone knows your business and you know everything about your neighbors. Even the stuff you don't want to know and desperately wish you didn't."

The bartender laughed. "Sounds like fun. I already know way too much about most of my friends and family. My name's Joe, by the way."

"Then you'd fit right in, Joe. I'm Noah."

"Are you hungry?" The bartender slid a plastic menu in front of Noah. "You can order anything from the dining room right here."

"I'm not sure–"

Noah didn't get his entire thought out of his mouth before it went completely dry, the words stuck in his throat. He couldn't seem to drag his gaze away from one of the women that had walked into the bar. The entire world had come to a standstill.

She was gorgeous, but not obviously so. It wasn't so much her looks that entranced him, but her genuinely happy smile and the way she carried herself, confident but not in an arrogant way. She was laughing at something her girlfriend had said and her entire face had lit up. She was so...alive, so animated, that the room practically vibrated now that she'd walked into it. It was as if everything had been in black and white but now it was a riot of color.

And all she'd done was enter a room and laugh. What witch-craft was this?

Noah had never had any trouble with the female sex. In fact, it was quite the opposite. Whether due to his last name or other more earthy attributes, women had come to him. He hadn't had to chase them down. Therefore, he'd never found himself in a romantic drought unless it was a self-imposed one.

He'd broken up with his latest girlfriend about a month ago and he'd been fine on his own since then. No loneliness. No eating ice cream and wallowing in self-pity. He'd welcomed the time to himself and had thrown even more energy than usual into his work on the family ranch. He hadn't been looking for a woman. At all.

But he couldn't deny that this one had caught his eye. There was simply something about her that intrigued him. Turning back to the bartender, he could still feel her presence even though he couldn't see her.

"I think I will order some dinner."

He wasn't fooling anyone, least of all himself. He'd been planning to eat in his room but now he wanted to stay here longer.

That's stalking. I'm a big creeper.

Noah rationalized it away by telling himself that it was more enjoyable to eat here in the bar talking to Joe than alone in his room. He was an extrovert, after all.

The woman and her friend had taken a table only a few feet away from where Noah was sitting. He could see them out of the corner of his eye. They ordered a round of drinks and some food to share.

This is pathetic. I'm acting like I never get laid.

Inwardly chiding himself at his curiosity, he tuned the two women out, gave the bartender his order, and then concentrated on the football game that was in the second quarter. By the time his food arrived, he'd completely forgotten about the woman. Mostly.

He could still hear her laughter every now and then along with the other female. Whatever they were talking about they were having a good time doing it. He glanced around the small bar and there were a few other patrons, mostly male, but they didn't seem to notice anyone else, either deep in conversation or heads down over their phone.

"Can I get you another beer?" Joe asked, wiping down the bar.

Why not? He wasn't driving. He only had to navigate back to his room and fall asleep. Maybe a third drink would help him sleep in a strange bed. He was getting old and set in his ways. He didn't like sleeping away from home.

He was just taking the first sip of his beer when he heard a voice at his left shoulder.

"Excuse me, can I get some more napkins? I spilled my water."

It was her. The woman he'd been looking at earlier. Her voice was soft and a bit husky. Her perfume teased his nostrils, something floral mixed with spice.

Joe grabbed a stack of paper napkins and handed them to her but also quickly came around the bar, towel in hand and ready to assist.

"Let me help you."

This time Noah did turn around and was surprised to see that the woman's companion wasn't sitting at the table. She must have left at some point when he was watching the game and eating. She and Joe quickly cleaned up the mess and carried the sodden napkins back to the bar where he disposed of them in an out of the way trash can.

"I'll get you another drink. It was just water?" Joe asked, already filling a glass with ice.

"Just water, thank you," the woman laughed, sliding onto a bar stool. "I don't even have the excuse that I was drinking. I'm just that clumsy."

"No damage," Joe replied with a grin. He slid her new beverage in front of her. "It's all good."

"Thanks for the help."

Instead of moving back to her table, the woman stayed in the seat next to Noah's.

"What's the score?"

Is she talking to me? She must be because no one else is around.

"Ten-seven, in the third quarter."

She squinted up at the television set. "Thanks. I can't see well without my glasses. They're in my room."

And just like that...they were talking to each other and she'd been the one to instigate it.

"You're welcome," Noah replied. "It's not that great of a game. Sloppy offense and marginally better defense."

She raised her brows and a smile played on her full pink lips. "Frankly, I wouldn't know the difference. I like to watch football but I don't know much about the game. I don't know the difference between a screen pass and a blitz."

"A screen pass is for offense and a blitz is defense," Noah explained, but didn't bother going into the finer details of the gridiron. She didn't appear to be asking for the information.

"That's more than I knew a minute ago." She sipped her water and her gaze flickered over him. "Here for business?"

His hand reflexively went to his knotted silk tie, so different than his usual jeans and t-shirt. "Yes, I am. Does it show?"

She nodded. "It does, but it wasn't a wild guess. I'm sure most of the people in this bar are here for business."

"Are you?"

"Yes, although I'm not sure if it was worth it or not. I won't know for days."

"You and your friend seemed like you were celebrating."

Her smile widened. "Were you spying on us?"

Shit. Noah could feel the heat in his cheeks.

"Of course not, but I could hear you laughing."

Did she believe him? He couldn't tell, but then she didn't seem perturbed about the idea, either.

"Tonight didn't have anything to do with business. Sandy is a friend from college."

Noah didn't know what else to say. He would offer to buy her a drink but she had a full glass of water in front of her. They ended up watching the game for a few minutes until the next commercial.

Why not?

"Can I buy you a drink?"

She held up the glass of water. "I've got one, thanks. Are you trying to pick me up?"

"What? No...Just...no."

The heat was back in his cheeks. This woman had brass balls, though, and he admired her spirit. His mother would have said she had gumption. Mom loved gumption.

Laughing, she shook her head. "Relax, I'm just giving you a hard time. You're a little uptight."

Uptight?

"Literally no one in my entire life has called me uptight," he replied. "My brother, on the other hand, he's uptight. I'm the laid back one."

"You have a brother?"

Noah chuckled at her innocent question. "I have three brothers but the one I was talking about is my twin. I'm older by seven minutes."

"There's...*two* of you? Are you identical?"

She appeared disturbed by that thought. He didn't blame her.

"Identical twins," he confirmed. "But no one has any trouble telling us apart. Easton wears suits every day and I'm usually in jeans. His hair is also cut much shorter than mine. Now...he's uptight."

Her gaze swept him again from head to toe, her gaze warm and appraising. "Jeans? You must have a casual job."

"I work on a ranch. I'd ruin this suit before sunrise."

"A ranch? You're not from Chicago, then."

"Montana. And you?"

"Denver, and I do have to dress up every day. I work in a bank. I'm quite jealous that you get to wear jeans."

With her long legs, she would look amazing in blue jeans. Today she was dressed in a black pencil skirt, white sweater, and black high heels. Her chocolate brown hair was coiled on the top of her head but a few stray curls had escaped and were resting on her cheeks. Noah couldn't help but wonder how long her hair was. He was a sucker for long hair. Long hair and amber-colored eyes.

"My name is Noah, by the way."

He realized he didn't know her name. And he wanted to. Badly.

"Noah," she repeated and he liked the way she said it, with sort of a sigh at the end. "My name is Libby."

A pretty name.

"It's nice to meet you, Libby."

"It's nice to meet you, Noah." She tapped the rim of her half-empty glass, their gazes meeting and lingering. There was…something between them. He could feel it. He wasn't an inexperienced kid. He was a grown man and he damn well knew when an attraction was reciprocated. "If the offer is still open, I wouldn't mind a drink after all."

The evening had taken an unexpected turn.

But he wasn't complaining in the least.

Chapter Two

IT WAS WELL after midnight. Libby and Noah had been talking and laughing for hours but now even the bartender Joe was beginning to yawn and glance at the clock. Closing time was twenty minutes away and he'd just warned them it was last call.

Noah couldn't remember the last time he'd closed down a bar. College, perhaps? Hell, maybe Jason's bachelor party but then he remembered that they'd ended up at his cousin's house by midnight, playing poker until the sun came up.

But tonight, he simply didn't want the evening to end and clearly Libby felt the same. Not once had she looked at her cell phone or suggested that it was getting late. They were having too good of a time getting to know one another.

She was smart with a wicked sense of humor, a combination that Noah found intoxicating. She absolutely struck him as a go-getter, grabbing life by the handfuls and living it to its fullest. So far, she'd told him that she'd studied rock climbing and had been a racecar driver for a day. The latter had been a birthday gift from her sister and brother-in-law, the former something that she'd always wanted to do.

She worked in the loan department of a bank and was determined to move up, which was why she was in Chicago, interviewing for a management training program at a major financial institution. She liked mint chocolate chip ice cream, pizza, and her favorite vegetable was sweet potatoes. She'd told him frankly that she didn't like to eat anything green if she could help it. She was a dog person; she liked reading more than television, and she hated hot weather.

She also smelled terrific and her skin was as soft as satin. He knew that because he'd brushed her hand with his at one point when she was talking about her first heartbreak. That simple touch had sent a rocket of electricity through his bones that he hadn't expected. He couldn't remember the last time he was this physically attracted to a woman but his hormones were in overdrive.

Not that he was letting Libby know that. He didn't want to be *that guy* who thought he was going to get lucky and act like a douchebag. He was going to be a goddamn gentleman even if it killed him.

Later in the evening, Noah had told her stories about growing up with three brothers and a bunch of cousins and she'd told him about growing up in the Midwest with her one sister and dad. Her mother had left when Libby was a teenager to *find herself*. Eventually she'd remarried and divorced more than once, only contacting her two daughters a few times a year. Dad had eventually remarried to a wonderful woman who adored the girls and they were one happy family now.

"You know absolutely everything about me now," Libby declared with a giggle, but not because they'd had too much to drink. They'd switched to ginger ale sometime around the end of the football game. "I have no secrets."

Noah shook his head. "Everyone has secrets."

"Nope, not a one. You know it all."

He doubted it but it he'd certainly learned a great deal about Libby tonight. One thing stood out among it all though...

He wanted to get to know her even better.

Denver wasn't that far. They could travel back and forth. They could make it work. He hadn't felt this much for a female in way too long. It wasn't just a physical thing, although he found her incredibly attractive.

He liked her. Genuinely, as a person and not just a potential bed partner. He'd enjoyed sitting and talking with her tonight more than his last several dates. Combined.

They had...*chemistry*. The awareness between them was real. He could feel the heat simmering just under the surface but neither of them had acknowledged it.

Sighing, she pointed to the clock on the wall behind the bar. "I think Joe wants to close up and go home."

Noah couldn't argue, although he wanted to. The evening had flown by far too quickly.

"I'll walk you to your room," he said, reality beginning to rear its ugly head. Their time together was over.

"You don't have to–"

"I want to," he cut in. "It's late and it would be less than gentlemanly not to see you to your door."

And he wanted to stretch out this night a few minutes longer. Get her phone number and make a date for tomorrow.

With a wave of thanks to Joe and a big tip, they both exited the bar and headed for the elevator. Libby had told him she was staying on seven and he was on five. It was only minutes later that they were standing in front of her hotel room door. They'd both barely spoken the entire way there, and with each passing second he'd felt the panic rising inside of him. His heart was beating far too fast and the back of his neck was warm. He couldn't let this woman slip out of his life. He'd only just found her, even if it had been by accident.

"How about dinner tomorrow?"

He had a late flight out but he could reschedule for the next morning.

She didn't answer right away, looking down at the hotel carpeting and then finally up at him. Her teeth had sunk into her lush lower lip and he could instantly see that her answer was going to be no.

Did I read this wrong?

I thought she was feeling the same way.

Disappointment crashed down and it was a real, physical pain in his heart. Wait…when did his heart get involved? It was far too soon for that.

"I have a flight quite early in the morning," she replied, her voice soft in the quiet of the hall. Most guests had gone to sleep. "I have a meeting at work late tomorrow afternoon that I can't miss."

Think fast. There has to be another way.

"Then how about an early breakfast?"

He'd pretty much thrown out his pride. It wasn't doing him any good at the moment.

Her lips were turned down and she looked as sad as he felt. "I have to leave for the airport by five. The dining room won't even be open."

Shit. Shit. Shit.

Don't give up.

"I really enjoyed talking to you tonight. We could exchange phone numbers."

He held his breath waiting for her verdict.

Her head tilted and she regarded him closely. "You want to call me?"

"I do." When she didn't respond, he started to get nervous, joking his way through the tension. "But maybe you don't ever want to talk to me again. I probably bored you to death."

"You didn't bore me to death," she said. "You're a nice man."

"That sounds like half a sentence. You're a nice man but..."

Pushing back a stray hair, she leaned against the door frame. "It kind of is. You're a nice man, Noah. But have you really thought this through? You say you want to call me. Then what? We talk on the phone. Send each other texts and emails. Then maybe at some point in the future we visit each other?"

She didn't make that sound good.

"Maybe. Is that so bad?"

He sounded defensive and he didn't mean for it to come out that way, but he was disappointed. Clearly, she hadn't felt the sparks that he had. This had all been depressingly one-sided.

Had it, though? Even now he could feel that awareness shimmering between them. He wasn't imagining this. It was real.

"Not in the beginning." She sighed and shook her head. "How can I explain this? I think you're a great guy. I really do, but I've done the long-distance thing and it didn't work. Believe me when I say that we'd both end up unhappy."

"Denver isn't that far–"

"But Chicago is," she broke in gently, this time reaching out her hand and laying it on his arm. His flesh burned where she touched and the cotton of his dress shirt didn't make a bit of difference. "I'm hoping to get this new job. That's why I came here. If I get it then I'll be working ten or twelve-hour days. Weekends as well. You said that you do that too, Noah. Let's face it. Our timing sucks. We have demanding jobs and soon we'll live even farther apart than we already do. Modern technology can only do so much."

Noah hated that she was making sense. He wasn't quite ready to give up.

"We could do it…if we wanted to."

"You think I don't want to?" Her voice broke and a silvery tear ran down her cheek. "Do you think that tonight has meant nothing to me?"

"I don't know." Honestly, he didn't know what to do or say. He'd never been in this position before. He'd never had to struggle too hard for what he'd wanted in life. Happiness, women, friends…they'd all come easily. "I just know I don't want you to walk out of my life."

He sounded frustrated because that's how he was feeling. He could see that same emotion reflected on Libby's face along with sadness and resignation.

"I don't want to walk out either but I'm trying to be real here." Their fingers tangled together and he couldn't help but hold on tightly, afraid that if he let go, she'd disappear as if she'd never been there at all. "Have you ever dated someone long-distance, Noah?"

"No," he bit out. "I haven't."

"I have. It's not easy. We were never together and we were in different time zones, so getting in touch wasn't easy either. It all started well enough with the best of intentions. But soon our calls became scarcer and then the travel plans we'd had suddenly had to be postponed because we were so busy. And that's when the resentment and the jealousy set in. He didn't know what I was doing and I didn't know what he was doing. Eventually we had to admit that it wasn't working."

"I would never resent you."

She stepped closer and he caught a whiff of her perfume. Or maybe it was simply her shampoo or body wash. He wasn't honestly sure but he'd remember that scent for the rest of his life. It was imprinted on his mind and if he ever smelled spice and flowers again, he'd most certainly think of her.

"You don't really know that," she chided, a small smile turning up the corners of her rosy lips. "We don't really know each other, although it feels like we do."

It did feel that way but she had a point. It was emotion, not logic that had him trying to strike a bargain.

"I don't know how to counter your argument. I'm just frustrated that I met you at the wrong time and the wrong place."

Her eyes were shiny with tears. "I am, too. Believe me, this isn't easy for me, either."

This time he did give in to the urge to reach out and tuck a silky stray strand of hair behind her ear. There didn't seem a good reason not to at this point. "Where does that leave us?"

She took another step closer, close enough that their bodies were touching. Just brushing really, and it sent an ache straight from his heart, down through his gut, and to his groin. His desire for this woman had grown until it was a real, living breathing thing that he could almost reach out and touch. If his thoughts were public, they'd be a flashing neon sign over his head declaring how much he wanted to kiss her. And more.

He wanted to reach out and pull her into his arms, capture her lips, and kiss her like there was no tomorrow. He wanted to know what she looked like in the throes of passion, and he wanted to hear his name on her lips when she tumbled over the precipice.

Looking down at her, he could see her lips trembling and he ran the pad of his thumb across their pillowy surface as if to soothe the hurt that they were both feeling. To his surprise, she didn't pull away but instead leaned into his touch, her lids fluttering closed for a long moment. The tension that had been building between them all night was now their jailer, keeping them both locked in place, neither one of them wanting to escape.

"Right here and now. That's all we have." Opening her eyes, her gaze locked with his, the awareness between them thicker than before. She held up her key card. "Noah, would you like to come in?"

The invitation was out of left field. He hadn't expected it. Sure, he'd hoped but he didn't really think…

Fuck, why was he even hesitating?

Because I want to make sure that she's asking what I think she's asking.

"Are you sure? I mean…are you asking me…?"

Her tremulous smile was his answer. "We only have tonight. We've been building towards this all night, haven't we? Am I wrong?"

No, she wasn't wrong, although he hadn't wanted to get ahead of himself. Make assumptions that weren't real. She was far more courageous than he was.

She took his hesitation the wrong way, however. "It's okay if you–"

"No," he said quickly, his decision made. "I do want to come in. Very much. I just wanted you to be sure."

She slid the key card into the lock. "I'm sure."

So was he. If they only had one night…he'd make it count.

Chapter Three

LIBBY'S HOTEL ROOM looked exactly the same as Noah's – one king-sized bed, one dresser, one television, one round table, two chairs, and a trash can – although hers was neat as a pin. Her half-filled suitcase was sitting on the rack in the corner and a second pair of shoes were tucked under it. The top of the dresser was empty except for the usual plastic ice bucket and glasses. The drapes were open, showing off the skyline of the Windy City. There were a few million people out there but only the two of them in this room.

Dropping her purse onto the dresser, Liz walked to the windows and switched on a lamp before closing the drapes.

"Do you want something to drink?" she asked, turning back to him. "I put a couple of waters in the mini-fridge."

She looked nervous, her lips trembling and her hands wrung together. Noah was nervous as well, but he didn't want her to think that she couldn't change her mind if she needed to. He wouldn't press this if she didn't want him as much as he wanted her.

"I'm fine," he replied, taking a tentative step forward. "But you go ahead if you're thirsty."

She peeked up at him from under her lashes as she kicked off her shoes. "I'm not thirsty, either."

He stopped in front of her, but he kept his hands at his side while trying to break the tension. "It's a little awkward, isn't it?"

He must have said the right thing because Libby smiled. A real smile that punched him right in the gut and left him breathless.

"It is. I mean...I don't really do this." Her eyes went round and she shook her head. "What I mean is that I have had sex, of course, but I don't make a habit of... Shit. I don't know what the hell I'm trying to say."

This time he did reach for her, pulling her close to his body. "What you're trying to say is that you don't go around inviting strange men into your hotel rooms. Am I right?"

Sliding her arms around his middle, she nodded. "That's it, although I wouldn't say that you were strange. You're a little goofy, sure, but strange?"

Laughing, Noah lifted Libby up in his arms, placing her on the bed so she towered over him. "Goofy, huh?"

Her fingers carded through his hair, the nails lightly scraping his scalp and sending a bolt of lightning straight to his groin. She was wearing a playful expression, although the tension was still there between them. Except that it had morphed from awkward to...steamy.

Damn, it was hot in this room. He needed to get rid of his clothes.

Better idea. Get rid of *her* clothes.

Sliding his fingers under her sweater, he found the warm, satiny skin underneath. Noah bared her midriff and then pressed open-mouth kisses on her abdomen before running his tongue along the waistband of her skirt. Her fingers tightened in his hair and she groaned when he delicately nipped at her belly button.

"Am I still goofy?"

His voice sounded strange even to himself. Far more gravelly and deep. Already he was hot, hard, and ready but if they only had this one night, he wasn't going to hurry it for anything in the world. He wanted to savor every single moment of being with this woman.

"Immensely," she whispered, her hands sliding down his neck and resting on his shoulders as she sunk to her knees on the mattress. "Really, really goofy. But in a good way."

All night long Noah had been thinking about kissing Libby. Now that they were face to face and away from prying eyes, there was no way he could restrain himself any longer. He leaned down and brushed his lips over hers a few times. She tasted of chocolate and coffee and he couldn't seem to get enough of her flavor. With a groan, she pulled him closer and pressed her mouth to his, their tongues immediately tangling and playing tag while their hands tugged at their clothes.

Her sweater easily came off over her head and his nimble fingers worked on the button of her skirt. In the meantime, she'd managed to unbutton his shirt and push it off of his shoulders and onto the floor, her haste making her clumsy. He took a step back and released the button on his pants, pushing them down and then off. The heat in her gaze as she looked him up and down made his cock ache even more. He was suddenly glad that he hadn't been slacking on the physical aspects of his job.

She liked what she was seeing.

Frankly, so did he. So much, in fact, that he wanted to see much more. Her sweater was long gone, leaving her kneeling on the bed in her skirt and lacy pink bra. What was it about a woman's delicate underthings that made a man crazy? The blood roared in his ears and zipped through his veins as he slowly helped her out of her skirt, revealing even more creamy skin inch by gorgeous inch, until she was in front of him wearing nothing but a couple scraps of satin and lace.

Libby smiled teasingly, hooking her finger into the waistband of his tented boxers. "Are you going to just look?"

Fuck, no.

He captured her lips and they fell back onto the bed, their bodies pressed together. Surrounded by her scent, he kissed his way over her jaw and down her neck to where her pulse beat rapidly. He licked the salty skin and wound a long, silky tendril of hair around his fingers.

Placing her hands on his chest, Libby pushed Noah up and then reached behind her to unhook her bra. Tossing it aside, she then slid her panties down her long legs and added them to the pile of clothes on the floor. Noah's mouth went dry at how fucking beautiful she was. The tight rose-colored nipples, the gentle dip of her waist and then the curve of her hips. She was so goddamned perfect and he didn't know whether to fall to his knees in worship or kiss every inch of her from toes to forehead.

He chose the latter, because honestly it was the most fun option.

His heart hammering against his ribs, he lifted her foot and dropped kisses on the arch and then up the calf, over the knee, nuzzling the spot where thigh met hip. Libby moved restlessly under him, her hands clutching the sheets in her balled fists. He repeated his ministrations on the other leg, wanting to imprint her on his memory, reminding himself again that there was a clock on their relationship, and they had to make the most of the time that they had.

Nudging her legs apart with his shoulders, he pressed baby kisses to the soft skin of her inner thigh until she was moving restlessly underneath him, needing him to touch her more intimately. Tentatively, he slowly pushed a finger inside of her tight channel, and then a second, loving how the muscles clamped down on him. She was hot and slick and so ready for him. He was painfully hard as well, the ache all the way to his lower back, but he'd promised himself that he would take his time. No rushing through this.

"Noah," she breathed so softly he barely heard her. Leaning forward, Noah gave her clit a lick, and her hips jumped at the contact.

Not letting her catch her breath, he lapped at the swollen button while his fingers found that sweet spot deep inside of her. Libby moaned her approval, her nails clawing at the mattress as he drove her higher and higher, until she finally fell over the edge, calling his name a few times. When it was over she lay there limp and breathing heavily, a curtain of hair covering her face.

Crawling up her body, Noah brushed her hair away and pressed a kiss to her full lips.

"That looked like fun."

Giggling she wrapped her arms around him so that they were skin to skin.

"It certainly was. I'd like to return the favor."

He desperately wanted to feel her mouth on him, but even more he wanted to be inside of her. As close as he was to coming, he couldn't take the chance. He slid a hand down her side, feeling the curves and dips.

"I need you now. I can't last much longer."

As confessions go, it wasn't the most romantic, but Libby didn't seem to mind. She ran her hands down his back and then back up, tangling in the curls at the back of his neck.

"Do you have something?"

Something. The euphemism for protection. He nodded and slid away for a moment to find his pants on the floor, rummage for his wallet, and extract two foil packets which he held up in triumph.

"Can I help?" she asked huskily as he tore at the square with his teeth. Together, they rolled on the condom and he had to snap his jaws together to keep from coming right then and there. Her soft touch was almost more than he could handle and his sharp hiss didn't go unnoticed. She moved her hand up and down until his balls pulled up tightly and he couldn't take it any longer.

With a ragged breath, he pulled away and rolled onto his back. "Ride me. I want to watch you."

Straddling him, Libby balanced herself by placing her palms on his chest. Never losing eye contact, she lowered herself onto his aching cock, little by little, until he was in to the hilt. She hugged him like a velvet glove, pure perfection, and he didn't move for a long moment, instead drinking in the sight of this beautiful woman. He couldn't believe he was here with her but it was real. All of it.

When she began to move, he couldn't hold back the moan that escaped from his lips. Sublime. Better than anything he'd experienced before. So fucking good. She swiveled her hips and a shot of lightning zipped up his spine. Their bodies slick with sweat, they moved un unison, finding their rhythm, until he couldn't take the pressure in his lower back any longer. It was simply too much pleasure, yet he'd never get enough of her at the same time.

He paced his thumb on her clit and circled it once...twice...three times. She exploded around him, gripping him like a vise until he too tumbled over the cliff. His orgasm felt like white hot lava running through his body and the world spun. He forced himself to keep his eyes open, not wanting to miss a minute of *her*.

Libby was...incandescent.

Her skin was shiny, her hair tumbled all around her shoulders, and her eyes heavy-lidded with passion. He'd never seen anything more lovely and he drank it in until they were both spent, their arms and legs tangled and their bodies damp and sticky. They cuddled together, not speaking for the longest time. Eventually he had to take care of the condom and while he was up, he grabbed a bottle of water from her mini-fridge, twisting it open and offering it to her. She drank down a few gulps and then handed it back before lounging against the pillows.

The bedside lamp was still on. In their haste, they'd never turned it off. He laid back against the headboard and she scooted closer, pillowing her head on his chest. His throat tightened with emotion as they cuddled together like old lovers. But they weren't even close. Tonight was all they had.

It wasn't a bit fair.

Noah wasn't a child. He'd long ago realized that life was rarely fair, and he'd made his peace with that. But he couldn't help but rail against an indifferent universe that brought them together and then ripped them apart so carelessly. In another time and place...they could have had something.

"I can order some room service if you're hungry."

Her softly spoken offer brought him out of his reverie. Libby was looking up at him, her expression solemn. She had to be feeling the same as he was. Neither of them were happy about this but it was what it was.

He didn't want to waste time eating food. He wanted to make love to her until he physically couldn't anymore. A glance at the bedside table told him they didn't have long.

"I'm not hungry for food."

His appetite was only for Libby, this amazing woman who had the audacity to make him feel more than he ever had before.

Chapter Four

NOAH HEARD THE soft sound of a zipper in the dark. Libby was closing her suitcase.

Breathing deeply, her scent invaded his lungs and swamped his senses, bringing their lovemaking flooding back. All the steamy images, the moans, the caresses played out in his head one by one. His palm pressed the sheets next to him and they were still warm. She hadn't been out of bed long.

He didn't know what time it was but there was no light shining through the slit between the drapes. The sun wasn't yet up. She'd already told him that she had to leave at five to catch her early morning flight. She had a meeting to attend and a life to get back and honestly, he did as well. It was simply that at the moment that life back in Montana didn't look as attractive as it had only a few hours ago.

Can one night change everything?

Noah had always doubted that his life could turn on a dime but here he was…different. Whenever he'd traveled before he couldn't wait to get home, couldn't wait to sleep in his own bed. But now he wanted to stay and spend more time with Libby, get to know her better. It was that same voice that was also urging him to open his eyes and say something. Anything. Just so she wouldn't leave quite yet.

Just a few minutes more.

He wasn't going to do that, however. Hadn't they said everything already? Even after they'd made love, their bodies cooling and spooned together, they'd tried to make sense out of their tenuous and brand-new relationship. A relationship that from the beginning had an expiration date. Eventually they'd both sadly recognized that they'd met at the wrong time and place. It had only been by chance after all.

If he hadn't hung around the bar after his business associates left...

And if she hadn't spilled her water...

And if he hadn't offered to buy her a drink...

And she hadn't left her glasses in her room...

It was a bunch of what-ifs.

They had met, of course, and he didn't regret it. Not for a second. The only thing he could wish for was more time, which he wasn't going to get.

He could hear Libby quietly slipping on her shoes.

He stayed very still, not wanting her to know that he was awake. Then there would be more awkward talking and he didn't want that. He didn't want to ruin this one amazing night that they'd shared. At one point, she'd joked that they were like Bogie and Bacall.

We'll always have Chicago.

Except that Noah wasn't Humphrey Bogart and Libby wasn't Lauren Bacall. And they didn't even have a song to fuck with him in the future when it played. They did have a football game and a shared slice of chocolate cake. Libby had picked up the dessert earlier in the day from a local bakery and they'd shared it in a post-coital bliss. Never had food tasted better.

Tensing, he heard the lock click and then the hotel room door opened, light spilling in from the hallway. His eyes were only partially closed but he could make out Libby's outline in the shadows.

This is it. She's leaving. I'll never see her again.

His gut twisted and he had to fight the urge to jump out of bed, to make a small scene, and then draw this fucking torture out further. They'd made their decisions. But dammit, he wanted it to be different. If he wasn't so cynical and jaded maybe he could have held on to the fantasy that somehow, some way they would have made it work.

I'm a realist.

The door didn't close. It stayed open far longer than it should have needed to. Libby was still standing in the doorway. Even if he hadn't seen her, he would have felt her presence in the room. He was that aware of her. And he'd known her less than twelve hours.

She didn't want to leave any more than he did.

His hands balled into fists of frustration and his teeth clenched together, his jaw aching. Whatever this was, it hurt like a bitch.

"Goodbye, Noah. Sweet dreams."

Her voice was soft. So soft he'd barely heard her whispered words and then the door clicked closed. She'd known he was awake the entire time.

Now he was alone. Just like before he'd met her last night.

But not like before.

Goodbye, Libby. Safe travels.

✦　✦　✦

NUMB. THAT WAS the only way that Noah could describe how he felt by the time he arrived at the airport for his own flight much later that same day. His business meetings had gone well and the trip would be viewed as a success when he returned home. He'd done his job and now it was time to leave Chicago. He had an eight o'clock flight out of O'Hare.

It was the usual rigamarole. Check in, then through security. He'd barely noticed the people around him, his mind elsewhere. He'd picked up a fancy coffee and settled into a chair, determined to keep his thoughts in the positive realm. He was going home, and although he'd arrive at his front door in the wee hours of the morning, he'd lay his head on his own pillow tonight.

Within a half-hour the waiting area had filled up as passengers queued for the flight. Noah kept his head down and his attention on the open laptop on his knees, composing an email to his twin brother Easton regarding all the particulars of the meetings he'd attended the last two days. It kept his focus where it needed to be. On the future.

"Is this seat taken?"

A woman's voice pulled his attention away from his work. An older woman, possible sixties or so, with graying hair and a big bag of knitting. She was pointing to the chair next to him. There weren't many empty seats left.

"It's fine," he replied, inching his own carryon closer to his legs. "No one is sitting there."

"Thank you," she said with a sigh, lowering herself into the chair with audible relief. She immediately pulled out her phone and tapped away at the screen. "I hate flying these days. It's all hurry up and wait. I was standing in the security line for over an hour."

That line had been particularly brutal tonight. This was one of the reasons Noah liked to travel light.

"At least our flight is on time," he said, keeping his gaze on his laptop. As nice as the woman was, he didn't want to get into a conversation. He wasn't in the mood to chat. "We'll get home before morning."

"That is good. At least, we're having a better night than those poor people." She nodded toward the televisions overhead. The airport had CNN on the monitors. "They have to be scared to death."

He glanced up and saw a banner on the bottom of the screen – *Twelve Hostages Held in Bank Robbery*

"What is the world coming to these days?" the older woman asked, shaking her head. Noah didn't get a chance to reply as the flight attendant came over the loud speaker and announced that boarding for the flight was about to begin. Since he was flying first class, he could board right away. A nice perk that tonight he appreciated more than usual.

He bid the lady a safe flight and boarded the airplane, stowing his carryon under the seat and getting settled. Buckling his seatbelt, he felt the engines rumble underneath him as the last of the passengers trundled down the aisle. To his relief, no one was sitting next to him for the flight and he wouldn't have to make awkward small talk with a stranger for three hours. What could he say if they asked him how his trip went?

Well...I met this amazing woman, made love to her, and then we parted, never to see one another again.

That was probably TMI for the average airplane passenger.

Had it even happened? Perhaps it was all a highly realistic illusion caused by too much hotel food and not enough sleep. Had Libby even been real? Had any of it been real?

Maybe she wasn't as wonderful as he remembered. Perhaps in her real life, she wasn't as interesting or funny or intelligent. Perhaps she hadn't really felt the same and was just humoring him. Maybe she did this all the time when she traveled, picking up strange men and making them believe things that weren't even true.

What if...what if she actually had a boyfriend, or even worse, a husband? She hadn't been wearing a ring but that didn't mean that there wasn't a man back in Denver. Maybe that's why she'd been reluctant to see him again. She was already in a relationship and he'd simply been the guy-on-the-side. What did he really know about her? Shit, he didn't even know her last name. Somehow, they hadn't shared that bit of information about themselves. It hadn't seemed important.

Except...she hadn't seemed to be lying. Her expressive features hadn't seemed to be hiding anything from him. On the contrary, her emotions had been laid out for his inspection just as his had been for her. She'd seemed sincere and he couldn't deny the mutual attraction. He'd felt it. It was real, even if none of the other stuff was.

Where did that leave him? Nowhere, of course. He'd never

see Libby again. Their paths had crossed for that one brief night and he'd have to be content with that. It was all they were going to get. It might have worked or it might not have. They might have gotten on each other's nerves and ended up hating each other. He'd never know. She was going to have to become a lovely memory tucked in the back of his mind, always perfect because she hadn't had a chance to be anything else.

Libby, a beautiful woman who in one night had captured a piece of his heart. Whether she was real or not, whether she'd been telling the truth or not...

She'd set the bar sky high for any other woman.

Chapter Five

Two years later…

LIZ HOLDEN WAS lost. Completely and totally. According to her GPS, she should be in front of her best friend's house but instead she was on a long, isolated stretch of road and she hadn't seen a human being for at least an hour.

Her best friend Mallory was getting married to some guy that obviously lived in the middle of nowhere and Liz was supposed to be one of three maids of honor. Because Mallory wanted all three of them and couldn't decide between them.

That was, of course, assuming that Liz wasn't permanently lost and that they didn't find her body in the spring. Mallory had warned her that Tremont was small and she hadn't been kidding. Liz had driven through it in minutes.

Now the Anderson family ranch was a different story. According to Mallory, the ranch was far larger than the town and that had proven to be true as well. The entrance to the ranch had been a long way back. She only hoped that she hadn't inadvertently driven off the property when she wasn't paying attention. There were a hell of a lot of dirt roads that led to heaven's knew where. So far, the Anderson ranch was...empty. Except for some cattle and trees.

And it was that emptiness that had unnerved her. The absolutely deserted roads had her white knuckling the steering wheel. Weren't there any people around here? Just where in the hell had her friend Mallory moved to? There were lots of cattle but actual human beings seemed scarce.

Now her GPS had taken her down a muddy dirt road and was telling her that her destination was on the right. The only thing on her right was a huge oak tree, thank you very much. Unless Mallory lived in it with her fiancé Carter Anderson and a few elves, this GPS didn't know what the hell it was talking about.

Now what do I do?

She could turn around and head back to the gas station where she'd filled up but that was about an hour away, or she could continue down this road. Surely, she would come upon a house or a human eventually? But first...

Liz pulled over to the side of the road and checked her cell phone. No messages, but she still had two bars of service, which was a surprise. There might not be any people but there had to be a cell phone tower somewhere hidden behind some trees or maybe a mountain.

Before she dialed, she ran her hand over the oversized bag in the passenger seat, reassuring herself that she could handle the unexpected. She could feel the outline of the bottle of pepper spray and her handgun – a Ruger 9mm. If anything – or anyone – unexpected happened, she was ready. She'd packed knowing she would be traveling alone and in sparsely inhabited areas.

"I'm lost," she said when Mallory answered the phone a moment later. "Completely and utterly lost. The GPS says I'm in front of your house but there's no way that I am."

"I'm looking out the front window and I don't see you, so I agree," Mallory laughed. "I know this sounds like a dumb question but can you tell me how you got to where you are? If Carter was home I'd just hand the phone to him. He knows every inch of the ranch and Tremont like the back of his hand, but he ran into town to grab all of us some dinner."

Liz was starving but if she wanted to eat, she had to get herself out of this mess. Slowly she recounted her drive from the gas station to her present location, hoping she didn't leave anything out.

"Uh, wow…You were there over an hour ago? It should be about thirty minutes from that station. Your GPS must have sent you the long way. But I do think that you're on the ranch. Does that huge oak tree have a heart on it with the initials 'EA + DF', by any chance?"

"I have no idea. I suppose you want me to go out and check?"

"It would help."

"I guess I don't have a choice," Liz sighed wearily. It had been a long day in the car and all she wanted to do was get to her destination before dark. "Hold on and I'll take a look."

Locking the car behind her and keeping her keys tightly in her hand, Liz threw her handbag over her shoulder and trudged over to the massive tree, its branches a canopy almost blocking out the sky. She didn't have to look too hard, though. There carved into the trunk was what she sought. A cheesy yet romantic gesture that no man had ever even considered doing for her.

Hallelujah. I must be close.

"I see it. Now what?"

Mallory quickly relayed the remaining directions and Liz ended the call and climbed back into the car. When she came to the fork in the road that Mallory had described she took the one going left and was delighted to see a charming two-story house at the end of the road only a few minutes later. There was a truck parked in the open garage and a light on in the front window that shone like a beacon in the waning light. Relief flooded her veins and for the first time all day, Liz felt her muscles relax. She hadn't realized just how tense she was until now.

Success. I made it.

Hoisting her purse over her shoulder, she left her suitcase in the car for the time being. From what Mallory had said, they wouldn't be staying here this week. Her weary legs climbed the front porch steps and she stabbed the doorbell once, surprised Mallory wasn't standing in the doorway or peering out the window watching for her.

The door flew open and a man stood there, his brows pinched together for a moment and then a look of shock grew on his far too-handsome face. It had been a long time but she hadn't ever forgotten that one night in Chicago, even when her life had fallen apart mere hours later.

It was a face she'd never thought to see again, although at times she'd questioned whether she'd met him at all. Perhaps their time together had simply been a figment of her imagination and she'd conjured him up out of thin air. So many times, she'd questioned her own sanity but now here he was. Standing in front of her.

The world tilted and spun and she had to grab onto the doorframe for support. She simply wasn't prepared for this and any words that she had on her tongue died an agonizing death. She couldn't speak and she wasn't sure that her heart was actually still beating in her chest. Her feet were glued to the wooden porch and she was shocked that she hadn't fainted dead away. It was a miracle she was standing upright.

"Libby?"

He was real. Not just her imagination.

If she stretched out her hand she could touch him.

He remembered her, and of course she remembered him, but that didn't mean that he'd thought about her even once all this time.

I've thought about him. Too many times.

"Libby?" he repeated, taking a step forward. Her instincts kicked in and she immediately took a step back. She didn't like people in her personal space. Not at all. "Is it really you?"

She reminded herself that he was shocked, too. Neither of them had any idea of what fate had in store for them today and he had to be as off balance as she was.

Is he happy to see me? I can't tell.

Better question…am I happy to see him? It's all so complicated.

It had been two years. She wasn't the same person that she'd been and a hell of a lot had happened in her life. She had to assume that it was the same for him. She tried to recall if Mallory had mentioned his name in the conversations they'd had about the wedding. Her friend had talked about the family she was marrying into but Liz couldn't remember her talking about Noah specifically. She had talked about Carter having twin brothers.

Noah was a twin. She remembered him telling stories about his brother Easton.

Two years. He'd probably met the woman of his dreams and settled down, maybe even had a kid by now.

And Liz? Not even close. She'd dated some but it always seemed like the men in her life were more about them than her. Mallory simply said that she had high standards, and Liz didn't disagree. She'd rather be alone than with the wrong guy.

Honestly, after Noah no one else had been able to capture her interest...or her heart.

He was staring at her and she realized that he was waiting for her to speak. How long had she been standing here like a statue?

"Yes," she managed to choke out over the lump that had taken up residence in her throat. She had so many emotions ricocheting through her body that she couldn't begin to make sense of them. "It's Libby. I mean...Liz. Most people call me Liz."

When she'd met Noah she'd told him the name that her family, friends, and colleagues called her, but in college when she'd met Mallory she'd been dubbed Liz for some unknown reason. It had stuck and later...*after*...she'd wanted to reinvent herself. She'd started using Liz with everyone.

"Liz." His brow was furrowed as if he was wondering if she was telling the truth. "Okay...Liz. I almost can't believe it's you."

Say something halfway intelligent.

"I'm here for the wedding."

It wasn't great but it was better than nothing. At least it was an entire sentence and actually made some sense.

His brows rose even farther. "The wedding? You know Mallory? Wait...you're Liz, her maid of honor? I don't understand. She said Liz was a pottery artist."

And Mallory had never mentioned Noah by name. But that was a completely different discussion.

"I am a pottery artist. I am also lost." She needed to get out of this situation. Pronto. Where was Mallory? Was she in the house? "Mallory told me to take the left fork and I'd find her house. Is she here?"

I'm not prepared for this. I need to get my shit together.

"This isn't Carter and Mallory's home. They live one road over. You took the left-left fork."

What in the ever-loving fuck?

This might be the strangest conversation Liz had had in a long while. They were talking as if nothing had ever happened between them. Maybe...to him...it hadn't been all that important.

"Oh." She glanced back at her car. "I guess I need to find my way there. Mallory is waiting for me. She's going to be worried."

As if on cue, Liz's phone rang and it was, indeed, Mallory. She gave Noah an apologetic look and answered, knowing that her friend must think she'd driven into a ditch.

"I'm fine," Liz said before even saying hello. "I took a wrong turn and I'm standing on Noah's front porch."

The way she said his name so casually had her flinching inside. She'd barely allowed herself to even *think* his name the last few years. Now she was saying it out loud like it was no big deal.

Her friend laughed. "Carter just showed up and pointed out that if you took the far left fork, you'd end up at his brother's house. Can you hand the phone to Noah, please?"

Why am I doing that?

"Sure."

Liz held out the phone to the man that had haunted her dreams for far too long. "She wants to speak to you."

Noah accepted the phone and pressed it to his ear. "Right. Of course. I'll make sure she gets there. No problem."

He held out the phone and she took it back, extremely careful that their hands didn't accidentally brush against one another. If he touched her...

She sure as hell wasn't prepared for that, either.

"I'll get my truck and lead you to Carter and Mallory. She wants to make sure you don't get lost and that's a possibility on the ranch, especially now that the sun is going down. Give me a minute and I'll get my shoes and keys. You should come inside."

No. She couldn't do that. Then this whole encounter might feel more real than it already did.

"It's okay. I'll wait here. You won't be that long."

Probably. I mean...it was just shoes and keys, right?

He opened his mouth and for a moment she thought he was going to argue with her, but then he shook his head and backed into the house, leaving the door wide open. Probably in case she changed her mind. She wasn't going to.

It took less than a minute and he was back on his front porch this time wearing shoes and holding a set of keys. She'd been so focused on looking at his face she hadn't even noticed that he was wearing faded blue jeans and a long-sleeved flannel shirt.

Just like he'd told her that night in Chicago. She'd easily been able to tell he wasn't a business suit kind of guy, although he'd looked sexy as hell in it.

He looked better in jeans, though. She walked behind him and she had a ring-side seat to watch his backside. If anything, he looked even better than he had and that was pretty fucking amazing, because she'd assumed over time that she'd built him up in her head. No one could be that sexy and handsome. Turned out she was wrong.

Noah Anderson could.

He was an Anderson. So much was falling into place. What he'd said that night, and what Mallory had said these last few months. Liz hadn't listened as well as she should and now she was paying the price. Blindsided. Like Wile E. Coyote running straight into a brick wall.

He pointed back down the dirt road. "Just follow me. We're going to take a shortcut."

Her brain had shut down and she was on automatic pilot. Nodding in agreement, she climbed into her economy sedan and fired up the engine. She followed closely behind his truck but there was a voice in her head that wouldn't let her alone. It was screaming for her to turn around and drive back to where she came from. Nothing good could come from this.

Then she thought about Mallory. Liz had made a commitment. Full stop. She'd see it through. Somehow.

Noah was the past. The *before*.

She couldn't allow herself to forget that.

Chapter Six

H E WOULD HAVE recognized her anywhere. That stubborn chin. Those whiskey-colored eyes and chocolate brown hair. Libby – no, Liz – had trimmed it to shoulder-length at some point but it was still as shiny and luxurious as he'd remembered.

She looked exactly the same.

So many nights after he'd come home from Chicago, he'd lain awake reliving their night together. The fact that he couldn't seem to evict her from his thoughts had often made him angry and frustrated but as time had gone on, he'd thought about her less and slept through the night more.

She'd never disappeared completely, though. She'd always been there in the back of his head whenever he dated another woman. He'd compare them and his girlfriend would never come out on the good end. Then he'd be pissed off at himself, but no woman could possibly be as wonderful as he'd built her up in his mind. At some point she'd changed from actual human being to a legend.

And now here she was. In the flesh. She was also going to be around for awhile as she'd come out to Tremont early to help with the last-minute wedding preparations.

What did that mean for…them?

It had been two years. The time had flown but a hell of a lot could happen in that amount of time. She could be engaged or dating someone or maybe she simply didn't have the memories of that night like he did. She might not remember it the same way. As in earthshattering. Frankly, her feelings may have never been as strong as his.

Do I really even know what I felt?

Noah didn't know but one thing was for sure. Libby-now-Liz was going to be here long enough for them to talk. He wanted to know everything she'd been doing for the last two years, and he wanted to tell her all he had done as well.

Face it. You want to find out if she's truly as great as you thought.

Fine, but isn't that normal?

Mallory and Carter were waiting on the front porch when they drove up. The two women threw themselves into each other's arms after Liz parked her car in the curved driveway. Carter ambled down the stairs and slapped Noah on the back, letting the ladies have their reunion.

"Thanks for bringing her. I had visions of having to send out a search party."

"No problem. I was just relaxing and watching some television."

"I brought enough food for an army. Come eat with us. Then you and I can have a couple of beers after the women leave."

Leave?

"Where are they going?"

Carter groaned and rolled his eyes. "Mallory has this bee in her bonnet about us not having sex for a few weeks before the wedding. It's supposed to make it more special on the honeymoon or some nonsense like that. So, Mallory and Liz are going to stay at Dizzy's old place. I'm not going to get a decent night's sleep while she's gone. I'm used to her snoring now."

"I don't know much about relationships but I don't think it's a good idea to mention that your wife-to-be snores. And you do too, by the way. Like a buffalo. That's why no one wants to share a tent with you when we go camping. It's one of the reasons, anyway."

"You snore, too," Carter retorted. "And I wasn't going to tell Mallory she snores. I was just saying that I'm used to sleeping with her. I think it's fucking romantic that I need her to sleep."

"You're a romantic fool. Or just a fool," Noah mocked. "I don't know how Mallory puts up with you."

"I wonder myself sometimes, to be honest."

The two women were done hugging and Noah was sure that he saw tears in their eyes. Mallory had talked about Liz quite a bit and how close they'd been in college, and then later when they were getting their careers started.

Liz. The pottery artist. Had Noah been lied to? He was beginning to think that. Had anything she'd said been the truth? Had he been played? He didn't want to think that he was the fool in this scenario.

Yes, she was actually real, but no, she wasn't who or what he'd thought. That fact was a bitter pill to swallow, and it gave him a pain somewhere in the region of his chest.

Mallory introduced Liz to Carter and Noah finally learned her last name. He couldn't help but watch closely, examining every expression on her face and every movement of her body. Was she a big liar? He wanted – no, needed – to know.

"Noah's staying for dinner," Carter announced. "So let's get inside and eat before it gets cold."

Liz appeared less than happy that Noah was going to be joining them for dinner. In fact, she was quite pale and her smile wasn't as genuine as he remembered. Whatever she'd expected today, she obviously hadn't been expecting him. They'd both been shocked.

Food was dished up and they all settled at the dinner table, Mallory to his left, Carter to his right, and Liz across from him. There was a hell of a lot he wanted to say but very little in front of his brother. With Mallory and Liz leaving for Dizzy's house later he wouldn't get the chance to talk to her. Normally he was a patient man, but in this situation he found that he couldn't keep his mouth shut.

"Mallory tells me that you're a pottery artist. That sounds fascinating."

Liz's head jerked up and her gaze ran from him to Mallory and back to him. "Yes, I am. It's very fulfilling work."

"You should see what she creates," Mallory gushed, setting her fork on her plate. "It's amazing. The colors are gorgeous."

This time Liz's smile was real. "I just might have made something for you and Carter."

Mallory's eyes went wide. "Is it in your car? Can we open it now?"

"How about after we eat?"

Noah wasn't done yet. "So how long have you been doing pottery, Liz? Seems like it would take years to perfect a talent like that."

Taking her time answering, Liz sipped her iced tea. "I've been doing pottery since I was a teenager but I only opened my own business about eighteen months ago."

"And she became instantly successful," Mallory bragged, clearly not aware of the tension that was building in the room. "She's amazing and people love what she creates."

Eighteen months? Had she not received the job offer in Chicago? Or had she received it and then found that she didn't like it?

"What did you do before that?" he asked, taking another bite of chicken. He wanted to keep his tone neutral, as if he was simply trying to politely get to know her.

Mallory grabbed the chicken platter in the middle of the table and held it in front of him, blocking his view of Liz.

"More chicken, Noah? I know how much you love the barbecued chicken from Ted's."

He had a fairly full plate.

"Uh, I'm good right now. Maybe in a few minutes."

Mallory wasn't going to give up, though. She set the platter down and picked up the pan of garlic toast. "How about some more bread then?"

What in the hell...?

"I'm good. Really." He emphasized the last word. She was acting strangely, giving him a look that he couldn't decipher.

"Carter, what about you? More bread or chicken?"

He'd never seen Mallory like this. She was acting weird and

she never acted weird.

Carter, who had a hollow leg, accepted the pan. "I could eat a little more, thanks."

Noah tried again. "So, Liz—"

"Carter," Mallory said loudly, interrupting what he'd been about to say. "Have you and Noah nailed down the bachelor party plans? What have you decided to do?"

Okay, she was officially acting like a loon. She wasn't going to let him speak, apparently. If his brother thought it was strange, he wasn't saying anything.

"Just a get-together. Pizza, beer, and poker. No strippers," Carter laughed. "I promise."

"Absolutely," Noah agreed. "No strippers. It's going to be really casual and low key. How about the bachelorette party? What do you ladies have planned?"

"Probably a movie night," Mallory replied. Liz had stayed strangely silent. She seemed content to be in the background of the conversation. Hardly the woman that had boldly spoken to him first at the hotel bar that night. "Just the girls. A few pitchers of margaritas."

The next half-hour went about the same. Every time Noah tried to speak to Liz or ask a question, he was interrupted by Mallory loudly changing the subject and Carter going along with it. If he'd had any ideas about her trying to fix him up with her best friend — and he really didn't — they would have been blown to bits by now. She didn't even want him to *speak* to Liz.

Except that didn't make a lick of sense. It would have if Mallory had known about Noah and Liz prior. But Liz had been shocked to see him so there was no way she could have told

Mallory about knowing him in advance of tonight. So something else was afoot here. He didn't like mysteries all that much.

Liz made a point not to make eye contact with him, keeping her gaze firmly on her plate for most of the meal.

When they finished dinner, Carter offered to clean up and do the smattering of dishes so the girls could head directly to Dizzy's house and get settled. Mallory continually put herself between Noah and Liz. There was no way he was going to have a chance to speak with her. Not tonight. But tomorrow was another day. He'd try again. And find out what the hell was going on.

Mallory hustled Liz out of the front door as quickly as possible, with barely a goodbye to Carter, leaving Noah to help with the dishes. He didn't mind at all, however, because it gave him a chance to speak with his younger brother. Perhaps he could shed some light on the situation.

Time to ask a few questions.

✦   ✦   ✦

"Do you want to talk about it?"

That was Mallory's question to Liz after they dumped their bags at the home they'd be staying in until the wedding. They'd made small talk the entire trip there but Liz had known that her friend had noticed her discomfiture. They'd spent four years as roommates, after all. Few people knew Liz as well as Mallory.

They'd changed into comfy pajamas and Mallory had poured each of them a glass of wine. Liz didn't like to use alcohol as a crutch but she sure as hell needed it tonight.

"I don't even know where to start."

"The beginning is the usual place. How about there?"

Liz rubbed at her temples. A nasty headache had bloomed there and it wasn't a mystery as to where it came from.

"It just all feels so surreal. Like it's not really happening."

If Liz went back to sleep right at this moment, would she wake up and it never happened?

"Now I'm really curious as to what is going on. You don't have to talk about it if you don't want to. I'm only trying to help."

"I know." Frankly, Liz was tired of needing help. It felt like the last two years were all about her friends giving and her taking. "It's not easy to talk about."

Where to start?

Her heart squeezed painfully in her chest as the memories crowded her brain. She'd rarely allowed herself to think about Noah. It was a luxury she couldn't afford.

"I guess I should start the story in Chicago."

Chapter Seven

❧

NOAH TRAILED AFTER Carter into the kitchen. His brother tossed him a dish towel.

"I'm just going to load the few dishes we have into the dishwasher. Can you wipe up the table and the countertops?"

Looping the towel around his hand, Noah leaned a hip against the counter. "Sure, in a minute. I wanted to ask you about Liz–"

"How about a beer?" Carter interrupted, looking more than a little harassed. Red dots had appeared on his cheeks and he was rubbing the back of his neck. "I have ice cream, too."

Okay, it was officially fucked up.

"I do not want a beer," Noah replied, his teeth gritted together so tightly his jaw ached. "I want to ask about Liz. Why won't anyone let me ask a question? There's something going on here and I want to know what the hell it is. And the first question is when did she change her name from Libby to Liz? The second question is did she ever work at a bank? Because that's what she told me two years ago and I foolishly believed it."

Carter's mouth had fallen open and he appeared to be having great difficulty trying to speak. Eventually he managed to croak out a question.

"Wait…you already know Liz? I don't understand."

"That makes two of us," Noah ground out. "Why won't anyone let me talk? No one would let me speak to her at all."

Scraping his fingers through his hair, Carter sighed. "Because Mallory doesn't want anyone asking Liz any awkward questions."

"I asked about her pottery. How is that awkward?"

"How about you answer my question instead? What were you talking about when you said Liz used to be called Libby and that she worked in a bank?"

It didn't look like Carter was going to answer any of Noah's questions unless he fessed up to his prior relationship with Liz. Libby. Or whoever she was. But it wasn't going to be easy to talk about it. He steeled himself for another unwanted wave of emotions.

"I do know Liz. I met her two years ago while on a business trip to Chicago. She told me her name was Libby and that she worked in a bank. From what I've seen today, those were lies."

"You never told me about this."

Of course not.

"You're my brother, not my therapist. Why would I tell you? You don't tell me about women you meet…or met, now that you're getting married. I had no idea that Mallory's Liz was the same woman I met in Chicago."

"Shit," Carter muttered under his breath. "I'm afraid to ask this question but I think I need to. When you say you know Liz…do you…*know* Liz? If you know what I mean?"

"That's none of your business," Noah replied sharply.

"That answers my question." Carter groaned and sat down at the small kitchen table. "I think you need to tell me just how you met Liz and why you think she's lied to you."

Noah sat down across from his brother. There was no delaying the inevitable any longer.

"I was having a beer after a meeting. Liz was there with a friend. She was in Chicago to interview for a management training program at a financial institution. At least that's what she told me that night."

But it all could have been a lie.

✦　　✦　　✦

"THAT'S THE WHOLE story," Liz sighed as she finished describing her heartache as she walked away from the hotel room that morning two years ago. "I took a cab to the airport and caught my flight back to Denver. I went into the office for my meeting...and well...you know what happened after that. Noah was the least of my problems then."

"I'm gobsmacked," Mallory confessed. "All this time..."

"Talking about it was too painful. I would have told you eventually but after awhile, it didn't seem important anymore. I wasn't ever going to see him again after all."

"Except that you have." Mallory shook her head. "You really had no idea? Nothing I said ever made you think it was him?"

She hadn't had a clue. If only she'd had. She would have been more prepared.

"We never told each other our last names. I don't know if it was intentional or an oversight, to be honest. Maybe we both thought it was more romantic if we were a little anonymous. He said that he worked on a ranch in Montana. I bet a lot of people can say that." Liz slumped against the cushions on the couch. "He thinks I've lied to him. I could see it in his face."

Not to mention the questions he'd been trying to ask.

Mallory rubbed her chin. "That bothers you? That he thinks that you're a liar?"

"Of course, it does. Do you want people to think that you're a liar?"

What a crazy question.

"Let me put this another way then. If Noah is just some guy from your past, why do you care what he thinks of you?"

Maybe the question wasn't that crazy after all. The answer was absolutely nuts, though.

"Because he mattered then," Liz finally said after a long silence. "I may have only known him a few short hours but he mattered. His opinion of me mattered, even though it shouldn't make a bit of difference. In truth, we barely knew each other. We were a blip on the radar of each other's lives."

"But he mattered," Mallory said softly. "You cared."

"I cared."

Two simple words but they carried so much meaning.

"And you never forgot him."

"Never."

Mallory chuckled. "I'm not surprised, to be honest. These Anderson boys pack a punch. It didn't take me long to fall for Carter, although our first date was much worse than yours with Noah."

"It wasn't a date," Liz replied automatically. "It was…Shit, I don't know what it was but I don't think we can call it a date.

Technically, it was a one-night stand."

The words tasted bitter on her tongue. She'd known that it couldn't be anything else and she'd gone into the situation with her eyes wide open, but she hadn't expected to still be thinking about him so long after that night.

"If you sleep with him again then it wouldn't be a one-night stand."

Wha–?

Mallory must have lost her mind. Clearly, she wasn't thinking straight.

"Are you suggesting that I seduce him?"

No. No way. She wasn't the same person she'd been. She only wished that she was.

"The way Noah was looking at you during dinner I doubt it would take much effort," Mallory snorted. "He looked like he wanted to eat you up with a spoon."

"No, he looked mad," Liz corrected, an image of Noah's face at the dinner table would be indelibly printed on her brain. "He's angry."

"He's just frustrated, and even if he is angry, he'll get over it."

Liz couldn't hold back her laughter at her friend's antics. "Don't ever go into the spy business, by the way. You were so obvious at dinner that you didn't want Noah to ask me any questions."

"I had to," Mallory defended. "Unless you're ready to tell him…"

"I don't know," Liz said with a shake of her head. "I feel like I've told that story a million times. Do I have to do it again?"

"No, you don't. But that's why I kept interrupting him. I wanted it to be your decision."

Mallory was giving Liz that look. She'd seen it for years, all the way back to their college days. It was the one where Mallory was disappointed in something Liz had done but she didn't want to be mean and say it out loud. When they were young it was usually when Liz would go out and party instead of staying home and studying. Now it was for a much different reason.

"You think I should tell him."

She didn't phrase it as a question because it wasn't one.

"It's not my decision to make. It's completely up to you."

"But you think I should. Just say it. You think I should."

"I think...that if Noah feels the same way about that night...he'd want to know. He'd want to understand."

That was the issue. The impediment in front of Liz.

Did Noah feel the same way about that night? She simply didn't know.

And she was afraid to find out.

✦　✦　✦

NOAH HAD TOLD his story and rendered his little brother speechless. That wasn't easy to do as Carter Anderson rarely was at a loss for words, but somehow Noah had managed it.

"Wow...just...wow," Carter finally said, grabbing two more beers from the refrigerator. "That's a hell of a story. You never heard from her again? Ever?"

"Never," Noah confirmed. "We didn't exchange phone numbers or email addresses. Hell, we didn't even know each other's last names. There was no way to get ahold of her if I'd wanted to."

His brother gave him a shrewd look. "You wanted to."

"There were times I thought about it."

A whole bunch of them, but Noah wasn't going to tell Carter that. Shit, he probably already knew.

"So you both made it impossible to contact one another because you didn't think the relationship would work? Do I have that right? Now fate has taken a hand and brought you two together again. Kind of romantic, big brother."

"Since when are you romantic?"

"I can be romantic." Carter sounded defensive, his voice going slightly higher. "In fact, I'm the fucking king of romance, if you must know. Screw you."

Groaning, Noah rolled his eyes. "Right. Sure. You're a regular Casanova."

"For a man that's been given a second chance, you don't act very damn happy about it. You're supposed to be the optimist in the family. Easton's the one that finds fault in everything."

Noah's twin Easton did do that, although he'd mellowed quite a bit since marrying Dizzy. She'd somehow sanded off his sharp edges and made him a better version of himself. She hadn't been trying. She loved Easton for who he was but being in love had changed him, and he appeared to be happy about it.

"A second chance?" echoed Noah. "You think that's what this is? Because that's not what this feels like. It feels like finding out that everything I thought was true was never real in the first place."

Closing his eyes, Carter loudly exhaled. "It was real, asshole. She didn't lie to you. She did work at a bank. As for the name

Libby, I've never heard Mallory call her anything but Liz but both of those are nicknames for Elizabeth, which is actually her name, so it isn't out of the realm of possibility that she introduced herself that way. I don't know all the things she told you, bro, but Liz isn't a liar. Mallory has good instincts about people, and she thinks Liz is amazing."

It helped. Knowing that Liz hadn't made up stories, stringing him along. The ache in his chest that had taken up residence when he'd seen her on the other side of his front door eased a bit and he was able to take a deep breath for the first time in hours.

"But she's a pottery artist now? That's a big change," Noah observed. "I guess she didn't get that job that she was interviewing for."

Which made him sad for her. He remembered the want in her tone when she talked about it, the sparkle in her eyes. She'd had big plans for her career and they hadn't worked out.

"But," Noah went on. "That doesn't answer my original question. Why didn't Mallory want me to talk to her? And don't say that it's my imagination. I'm not making this up."

"Mallory just wants to protect her friend."

"From me? Why would she need protecting from me? I don't want to hurt her. I just want to talk to her."

It didn't make any sense.

"You and Liz just need to talk to one another," Carter said. "That's what you need to do."

Noah couldn't agree more. He had questions and only Liz had the answers. The biggest question he had...

Was she everything that he'd imagined? Or had his memory fooled him?

He needed – no, he deserved – answers.

Chapter Eight

LIZ HAD TOSSED and turned most of the night, her mind not letting her rest. She couldn't get the images of Noah out of her head – in Chicago and then across the table from her last night. Mallory thought she should tell Noah about her life but she wasn't quite sure that was the right thing to do.

Just what did their time in Chicago mean?

She needed to know. Once and for all. Had she built it up in her memory and made it more than it was or had he felt the specialness of that evening the same way she had? She'd thought about him so many times over the last two years, especially when it felt like there were no good people in the world.

"Hey, are you almost ready to go?" Mallory called from the hallway. Liz was ready and dressed to go to breakfast. All she needed was a little lipstick. "My stomach's grumbling and groaning."

"I think I'm ready," Liz said, shoving the tube of lipstick into her oversized bag, along with her wallet and keys. "I'm starved, too."

Mallory's head popped into the doorway as Liz loaded up her bag. "Then let's get going. They might run out of food before we get there."

"That probably won't happen."

"Just in case..." Mallory stepped in the room and frowned, reaching out her hand to rest on Liz's arm. "What are you doing?"

Liz looked down at her handbag in confusion. "I would think it's self-explanatory. I'm getting ready to go."

Her friend pointed to the interior of Liz's purse. "Can you explain what I just saw you doing?"

Ah, I see where you're going here.

It appeared that Liz and Mallory were about to have a serious conversation.

Liz pulled the stun gun from her purse and held it up. "You mean this?"

"And that," Mallory said, pointing to the handbag again.

Laying the stun gun on the bed, Liz retrieved the handgun from her purse and set it next to the stun gun. She'd learned to shoot it about eighteen months ago. "This?"

"Yes, let's start with that."

Liz didn't answer right away, instead walking over to her suitcase on the floor and pulling out a can of pepper spray. "Or did you mean this?"

Mallory's face paled. "Jesus, Mary, Joseph, and the camel, you're a walking arsenal. What's going on? You're loaded for bear and it's just a wedding."

It was funny how Liz hadn't imagined this moment. She'd swept it from her mind like so many other unpleasant and thoroughly stressful things that she didn't want to deal with. She'd hoped that Mallory wouldn't notice but she should have known better. Mallory noticed everything.

"You can't be too careful," Liz replied, tucking the pepper spray back into her suitcase. "I just want to be able to protect myself, that's all."

Mallory held up her hands in surrender. "Listen, I totally get that and this is Montana, my friend. No one is going to think that you're wrong for carrying a gun but I'm just shocked to see you do it. You were pretty anti-gun for self-protection when we were in college."

Liz shrugged carelessly, not meeting Mallory's gaze. "Things change. People change."

"I guess they do. I was simply surprised, that's all."

Listening for any sort of censure in her friend's tone, Liz placed the stun gun back in her purse. "I'm sorry I surprised you. I don't want you to worry that I'll do anything stupid like shoot my foot. I've taken classes and I know how to handle a firearm. I have a permit."

"I'm sure you do."

For some reason, she couldn't let the subject die. She wanted to explain until she was sure Mallory completely understood.

"I'm not going to be someone's victim. I'm prepared."

This time.

Mallory's face crumpled, her eyes filling with tears which only served to make a lump grow in Liz's throat. She hadn't wanted to become emotional. She'd cried far too many tears and she was tired of it.

"Liz, honey...this wouldn't have made any difference." She waved her hand toward the purse. "You know that, right? It wouldn't have helped."

You don't know that. Not for sure. Neither of us do.

"I could have–"

"No," Mallory said, her tone firm. "It wouldn't have made any difference. Where was your purse? In your desk drawer? Were you even at your desk?"

No, I was in the conference room.

Liz had played out the scenario in her head a million times, each one just a bit different than the one before it. Sometimes she was even victorious.

"I might have been able to do something," she finally said. "Maybe…"

She didn't know what else to say. The dubious expression on Mallory's face said it all. She didn't believe a word of it.

"You had a security guard, right? He was trained and he wasn't able to do anything."

"I know that."

Liz did know. But in her head at two in the morning, it didn't matter. She only knew that she was compelled to protect herself. She never wanted to go through that again. She wasn't sure she'd survive the next time.

Tentatively, as if afraid her friend would bolt, Mallory reached out her hand and placed it on Liz's arm. It felt warm and comforting but it didn't calm the churning in her gut or silence the annoying voices that told her she should be afraid. Doubt and fear had become her constant companions. The friends she could count on to be there for her whenever she was all alone.

"It was awful but you survived. *You survived it*, Liz. No one got hurt and everyone walked out alive."

Liz would have argued that many people had been hurt, but the wounds weren't the kind that you could put a bandage on. They were deeper inside and far more insidious.

"I know you're right."

It was logic, after all. She couldn't argue with logic. All she had were her emotions and they were all over the place, but extremely powerful.

Sighing, Mallory pulled her in for a hug which Liz returned. She'd missed her friend. Talking on the phone or Skype wasn't the same.

"Knowing I'm right doesn't make any difference, does it?" Mallory asked, resignation in her tone. "You're still scared."

"I don't like that word very much. I'm...cautious. I think I should be. The world is a dangerous place."

Mallory stepped back and shook her head. "Actually...it's not. Violent crime isn't going up. It's going down. The chances of something bad happening to you again are astronomical. Like you have more chance of being struck by lightning."

Liz gave a shaky laugh. "Statistics were never my strong suit."

"Are you still seeing your therapist?" Mallory asked softly, although there was no one to overhear.

"She moved to another state about eight months ago because her husband got a new job. I haven't found a new one yet."

I also haven't really looked, either.

"Maybe you need to search a little harder."

That awkward sentence had Liz smiling. Her friend was so sweet.

"That's the nicest way possible to tell me that I'm batshit crazy."

"You're not crazy," Mallory denied. "But I worry about you. I don't think this paranoia is healthy. I can totally get behind carrying one of these weapons, but all three? You only have two hands."

"I'm not paranoid. I'm cautious. There's a difference."

"Okay, you're cautious. I just don't want you to ruin your life worrying and waiting for something bad to happen to you. That's no way to live."

Living? Liz couldn't say that she'd been living life to the max lately. Mostly, she'd been existing. She'd been better in the last year but she wasn't the person she was before.

It all came back to the *before*... Now she was living in the *after*.

When she didn't say anything, Mallory pulled her in for another hug. "Please don't be mad at me. I just want to help you."

"I'm not mad." Liz pushed the words past the lump in her throat. "I could never be mad at you. It's just...everything is different now. I wish I could go back in time but I can't. I have to deal with the here and now but it's not easy."

"I'm here for you. I'll always be here for you."

"But that's not why I'm here," Liz protested. "I'm supposed to be here to help you."

With the last-minute wedding details, of course. Not with mental health issues.

"Maybe we can help each other. That's what friends do."

It couldn't hurt, and she'd never been one to turn down a genuine offer of help. Heaven knew, the last two years hadn't been easy.

"I may take you up on that."

"I'll hold you to it, but we can't do anything on an empty stomach. Let's go get some breakfast."

That was a plan that Liz could support. Coming here may have been the best thing that she'd done in a long time. She just couldn't stop wondering, though...

What if...she hadn't taken that early flight back to Denver? What if she'd stayed with him?

Then her *before* and *after* might have been very different. And so much better.

✦　✦　✦

SUNDAY DINNER AT the Andersons. Liz had heard a few stories from her friend but this was going to be far more stressful than a simple meal. Mallory had tried to prepare her but the only thing Liz could think about was that Noah would surely be there. She'd have to see him and yes, she was going to have to speak to him. After discussing it over breakfast, Liz was convinced that they needed to talk.

"The whole family will be here," Mallory said for the sixth or seventh time that morning. They'd pulled up in front of the main Anderson house where the parents lived and the minute her friend put the car in park, Liz's heart had almost galloped out of her chest. Plus, there was stress sweat pooling on the back of her neck and under her arms. She had to resist the urge to give herself a sniff. "Do you remember what I told you about them?"

How could she forget? Mallory had drilled her over bacon and eggs.

"There are two Anderson brothers," Liz recited. "David and Joe. They both married and had children. You're marrying into

Joe's side of the family. Noah and Easton are twins and the oldest. Then Shane, and finally Carter. On David's side, there's Travis, Jason, Westin, and Leann, the only female. Did I get it right?"

"You got it," Mallory said with a quick thumbs up. "I won't go into their wives' names because your brain might explode, but trust me when I say that it will be a full house. Both sides of the family don't always eat together on Sunday but they are today."

"One big happy family."

"Pretty much. I'm told there are some cousins coming to the wedding that I haven't met yet. They run a different part of Anderson Industries."

"Anderson Industries," Liz repeated. When Noah had told her that he worked on a ranch she hadn't pictured him a titan of business. If anything, she'd thought he was a ranch hand of some sort. Like on television. "It sounds…big…and important."

"It is big and important."

"How big is big?"

"Big." Mallory's expression was solemn. "Just…big. Whatever you're thinking is big…it's bigger."

"That's pretty big."

"It is. And intimidating but the Andersons are a down-to-earth family. Thank goodness. I never got the vibe that they thought I wasn't good enough for their son." She giggled and slapped a hand over her mouth. "If anything, his brothers have made suggestions that he's not good enough for me. I told you he had something of a reputation when we met. He was quite the heartbreaker."

If the rest of the family looked like Carter and Noah, Liz was positive that the Andersons had broken plenty of hearts.

I don't want to talk about my heart.

"He looked like a devoted fiancé last night."

"He is. We both are. Now are you ready to meet them? Brace yourself, because there's a lot of them."

Liz came from a much smaller family. She had a sister that she talked to once a month and saw at the holidays. Her parents were divorced and her dad had remarried. There were a few cousins but she rarely saw them except on social media. Her grandparents had passed away when she was in high school. She loved her relatives. All of them. She just didn't spend much time with them. Getting together on Sundays for dinner was an alien activity. She hadn't eaten Sunday dinner with her parents even back when she'd lived with them. They'd all had their own lives.

They were climbing the front porch steps when a terrible thought occurred to Liz. Panicked, she tugged on Mallory's arm, delaying the inevitable of going inside.

"Do you think Noah told his brothers? Do you think they all know?"

Liz was mortified at the thought of everyone staring at her and knowing that she and Noah had a past. She didn't yet know what that past meant to him…if it meant anything at all.

Mallory frowned for a moment and then shook her head. "I think he probably told Carter last night, but I doubt he told everyone. The brothers are close but they don't talk over every single thing with each other. I'm guessing that he wants to talk to you first."

Talk. Yes, they needed to talk.

Except she still didn't know what to say. She'd had all morning to think about it and she hadn't made much progress.

How do you ask someone if they'd fallen in love?

Chapter Nine

NOAH HAD CHUGGED two glasses of water and almost sweat through his blue button down shirt. Nervous didn't even begin to cover what he was feeling at the moment. Liz – it was still hard to get used to calling her that – would be walking in the door any minute. He had a million questions that he wanted to ask. Would she answer any of them? Last night he'd convinced himself that he deserved to have his questions answered but in the cold light of day he wasn't so sure. They'd had one night together and she hadn't promised him anything.

Liz owed him nothing.

By the same token, he could say the same. He didn't owe her anything either, but that didn't make him want to stay silent. He was going to try and talk to her today. If only to clear the air between them. They were going to be spending time together and he didn't want his past affecting his brother's wedding.

Carter peered out of the living room window that overlooked the front yard. "Mallory and Liz are here."

Noah stepped forward but his brother blocked his path. "I know you want to speak to her, and you should, but give her some breathing room. Let her meet everyone and settle in. There will be time after dinner. You can take her out to the gazebo and talk to her privately there."

The Anderson Gazebo. It was practically an institution all its own. How many romances had been sparked in that wooden structure? Too many to count, Noah was sure. He'd done his share of kissing in it but most of that was when he was younger. Some Andersons said that the gazebo was a magical place. Easton had proposed to Dizzy there and she'd said yes. That was pretty miraculous.

I could use some magic. Any bit of help would be good.

"Fine," Noah replied with reluctance. He'd been waiting for two years but an hour or two more wouldn't make much difference. "I don't want to make her feel uncomfortable."

Carter just grinned. "She's going to feel uncomfortable until she gets used to all of us. You know that takes some time. Let her get her feet under her. We're a big family and can be overwhelming."

There was no way Noah would ever admit it but he'd thought about this moment a few times. All those what ifs. If Liz had stayed in Chicago with him that day. If they'd tried to make long distance work. If he'd introduced her to his family as his girlfriend. When he'd imagined it, it hadn't been nearly this stressful. They'd been happy and smiling and in love.

I am a huge sap.

He did, indeed, feel for Liz when she and Mallory entered the house. A barrage of people descended on them, and there was no way she was going to be able to remember all of those names, let alone match them to faces. She'd told him that she was from a small family and he'd had the idea that they were rather sedate and quiet. In other words, completely the opposite of the Anderson clan.

Carter and Mallory stood on either side of Liz, keeping the family at bay as they all introduced themselves, one after the other.

"Aren't you going to say hello to our guest?"

The question came from his mother, who was giving him a look that said she thought he was being rude. No matter how old he was, she was still his mother.

"Actually, I met her last night." Simplicity was the way to move forward here. "She ended up at my front door instead of Carter's."

"I hope you helped her find the way."

"Of course, I did, Mom. We all even had dinner together before she and Mallory left for Dizzy's place."

His mother smiled. "That's nice. I've heard wonderful things about Liz. She's quite attractive, don't you think?"

Really, Mom? You're not even subtle anymore.

Kathy Anderson only had one child left unmarried – once Carter tied the knot – and she could hardly stand it. She'd been giving him broad hints for months that had become broader and less disguised as time had gone on. Frankly, Noah expected her to sign him up for online dating any day now.

"She's incredibly attractive," Noah agreed, because…he did agree. Wholeheartedly.

"And single," his mother added.

Single? How did she know that and he didn't?

"Are you sure, Mom? How do you know?"

Sighing, Kathy nodded toward where Liz was meeting West's

wife Gigi. "Because Mallory mentioned that Liz wasn't seeing anyone. We were doing the wedding reception seating chart and I asked if Liz had a plus-one. Mallory said that Liz broke up with someone a few months ago."

Leave it to Noah's mother to find out the dating status of Mallory's maid of honor.

"Are you trying to fix us up, Mom?"

A smile played on Kathy's lips. "I'm just making a comment."

The last thing Noah wanted was for his mother to play matchmaker. Not when she didn't have all the facts.

"Liz is a lovely woman and I do want to get to know her better." He raised his eyebrows and gave his mother a warning look. "No interference, please."

Kathy snorted in reply. "I am not the interfering type. You're a grown man and can handle your own love life...such as it is. I'm only saying that Mallory has nothing but wonderful things to say about Liz. She's a pottery artist. Did you know that?"

This conversation had taken a surreal turn.

"I did know that."

"She makes functional pottery, meaning that they're not just for show. You can use them."

"I didn't know that."

"She's very talented. Mallory showed me some pictures from Liz's website."

He hadn't known Liz had a website but if he had, he would have already checked it out. He could practically slap his own forehead.

The internet. Christ on a crutch. He could have looked Liz

up online and found out all sorts of information now that he knew her last name.

I'm as dumb as a rock.

Easton would have thought of looking Liz up last night. He'd always said he was the smarter twin, and Noah rarely argued with him about that point since he could always pull the *older brother* card. Seven minutes might not be much but it was enough to torture Easton for the rest of his life.

As usual, the females disappeared into the kitchen while the men sat in the living room and talked. After dinner, the roles would reverse and the men would be on cleanup duty while the women lounged and relaxed. The only difference was in the last few years the men had also taken on the additional responsibility of watching the children while the meal was being cooked. Most of the Anderson brothers had kids now, hell, even Carter and Mallory were already talking about trying for a baby quite soon.

Noah was the last man standing. Most of the time that didn't bother him in the least. He'd rather be alone than be with the wrong person. But every now and then, he had to admit that going home to his empty house was becoming less and less satisfying.

Had that all started when he'd met Liz? He didn't know for sure.

Joe Anderson slapped Carter on the back as he handed him a whiskey. "Are you ready, son? It won't be long now."

Noah's youngest brother prided himself on being a modern groom, enthusiastically taking part in the wedding planning and eschewing the old stereotypes about men being scared to tie the knot. Carter couldn't wait to be married to Mallory.

"I've been ready for months," he declared. "Mallory, too. I already feel married so the ceremony is just a formality."

"It changes things, son," Joe said solemnly. "I know you don't think things will change but they will. Those vows make it different."

"Makes it better," West replied, giving Noah a pointed stare. "It's the foundation that you can build on."

It seemed no one in the family was going to be subtle anymore.

"If you have something to say, West, you should just say it," Noah said, a relaxed smile on his face. Taking crap from his brothers and cousins was a well-known sport in the Anderson family. "It's not like you to beat around the bush."

West shrugged, handing a discarded toy car to his toddler son. "Okay, I'll be direct. You're becoming a real pain in the hindquarters, cousin."

"Hindquarters?" Noah sputtered with laughter. "That's an interesting turn of phrase. I know you haven't been hanging around the ranch lately."

West nodded toward the kids who were playing toy cars by the window. "Gigi told me that if I teach our second son the same words I taught the first one – accidentally, I might add – I'll be sleeping on the porch until Christmas. It's cold on the porch."

"Okay, I'm a pain in the...*hindquarters*. I'm not sure what that has to do with wedding vows."

"Marriage will mellow you out," West pronounced. "Look at Easton. He was wound tighter than an eight-day clock and headed straight to becoming Ebenezer Scrooge in *A Christmas*

Carol. But then he fell in love with Dizzy and it all changed. She has him juice cleansing, mediating, and doing yoga. He's never been more serene."

Noah's twin didn't look like he appreciated being a cautionary tale. "I wasn't even close to being Scrooge. And what about you? You had a terrible reputation with women until Gigi came along."

Shane chuckled and refilled his whiskey glass. "We all had our issues."

No, they didn't.

"First of all," Noah said to no one in particular. He'd immediately noticed that no one was coming to his defense. "I don't need to mellow out. I'm relaxed and laid back. I've always been that way. Second, I don't have a bad reputation with women, and third, I don't have any issues. You all might have had issues but I don't. I'm incredibly well-adjusted and normal. For this family. Oh, and fourth, I don't appreciate being ganged up on just because Carter found a woman."

"To be fair, we always thought he'd be the last to get married," Shane said. "He was hardcore single."

"Actually, I thought Travis would be the last," Noah said turning to his cousin who had sat quietly drinking his whiskey the entire time. "Are you going to sit there and let them talk to me like this? I thought you were my friend."

Travis didn't answer immediately, unfolding his long body in the chair to stretch out his legs. "To be honest, I thought I'd be the last to get married as well so I can't argue with you there. As for you being a pain, I have to also admit that I agree with West. Lately, you've become...impatient. More tense. You weren't like that in the past but we've definitely seen a change in the last year or so. We're a little worried about you, that's all. After the wedding, you should take a vacation from the ranch."

"Maybe the last two years," Carter piped up. "I wonder what changed around that time to make you this way?"

His head swiveling toward his younger brother, Noah shot him the stare of death.

"I am not more tense," Noah denied loudly. Everyone was royally pissing him off.

His mother stuck her head out of the kitchen. "Is everything okay out here?"

Shit.

Her brows rose when they were all quiet. "Well, this is quite interesting. Do I need to come out there?"

"No," Noah answered quickly. "We're just debating some-thing."

"Who's winning?"

"I am."

West snickered and Carter coughed, covering up his laugh-ter. Travis, Jason, and Shane were laughing as well. Only Easton and his dad had a straight face but they were amazing actors. Easton could have taken up professional poker and won millions.

"You'll have to finish later," his mother said. "Dinner's ready. Go wash up."

Stomping upstairs to wash his hands, Noah grumbled under his breath. He wasn't tense or cranky or anything else. He wasn't the one that had changed. They all had. He was the same easygoing guy he'd always been, and always would be.

Nothing bothered him.

Except maybe one beautiful woman on the other side of the kitchen door. He had to talk to Liz and tell her that he'd never forgotten.

✦   ✦   ✦

LIZ HAD GROWN up in a small family so gatherings this large were foreign to her. Everyone was talking at the table and although there were no angry voices it did get loud several times. It wasn't bad, it was just…different. By the end of the meal, she'd found that she actually sort of liked it. It was easy to see that the Andersons were loving and close, even if they didn't always completely agree with one another about whether it was going to rain tomorrow.

Apparently, weather was a big deal in Montana.

"The men do the cleanup," Mallory said when dinner was over. "We get to sit down and relax."

That's what Liz had been told earlier and it appeared to be true. The men immediately went to work clearing the table and the women were shooed out to the back porch with glasses of wine. It was a beautiful sunny day, not too warm and not too cool.

"Do you think the weather will cooperate for the wedding day?" Mallory asked wistfully, leaning against the porch railing. "Can we be that lucky?"

"In many cultures, rain is considered to be good luck," Dizzy replied. "It symbolizes fertility, cleansing, and renewal."

"It also makes big mud puddles," the woman named Aubrey said with a laugh. She was married to Travis and she was absolutely drop dead gorgeous, as was her sister Gigi, who was married to West. Liz felt like a ragamuffin next to them. "The kind that get the hem of your big white dress dirty. Let's pray for sun."

"True," Dizzy said with a giggle. "But I stand by my statement. Rain is good luck. What do you think, Liz? Rain or sun for a wedding?"

Liz didn't get the opportunity to reply. The back door swung open and Noah stood in the doorway. "Can we talk, Liz?"

All the ladies went silent. The heat rising in her cheeks, Liz cleared her throat and nodded. Words had escaped her at the moment. She'd known that they needed to talk but she hadn't thought it would be so soon.

Might as well do this. Dragging it out won't help.

She followed Noah down a tree-lined path to a lovely gazebo in the center of a clearing. They were close enough to the house that she could still see the women sitting on the back porch, but far enough away that they couldn't hear anything that was being said.

"This is pretty," Liz remarked, settling gratefully onto one of the benches. Her legs had been trembling so badly that she'd been afraid they might give out.

I'm that nervous.

And awkward.

"Our parents built it when they built the house," Noah answered, settling himself next to her. He was close enough that she could feel the heat of his body but they weren't touching. She had the strongest urge to reach out and place her hand over his. She didn't do it, however. That tension and awareness she'd felt last night was back with a vengeance, and after months of trying to feel as little as possible it was knocking her off kilter. "A lot of family history has gone down in this gazebo."

"Good or bad?"

She didn't know why she asked. She was mostly trying to make conversation.

"Mostly good." He took a deep breath, his hands gripping the wooden seat so hard that the knuckles were white. It was a relief in a way…to know he was nervous, too. "We need to talk, Lib– I mean, Liz. I don't know how you feel about–"

"Yes," she blurted, trying to ease the tension between them. "Yes, we need to talk."

He seemed to relax slightly; the set of his shoulders less rigid. This wasn't easy on either of them. She had so many questions but she didn't know where to start, or even if she should even ask them. Maybe it was far too late and it didn't matter anymore.

It matters to me.

She waited for Noah to say something but he seemed to be having a difficult time finding the words he wanted to say. It was in her nature to be uncomfortable with silences, but she forced herself to stay quiet while he organized his thoughts.

"It was a surprise to see you at my door last night," he finally said, his gaze on the wooden planks at their feet. "Frankly, it was a shock and I've barely recovered. In a way, I still keep thinking that I'm going to wake up and all of this was some crazy dream."

It was a shock for me, too.

His gaze swung up and their eyes met, sending a jolt through her system. Intense. That was the only way to describe it.

"I'm guessing you were shocked, too. Neither of us knew…"

Liz finally found her own voice. "It was a surprise. I never thought I'd see you again."

He turned his body so he was facing her, his arm on the back of the bench just inches away from her shoulder. The craving for his touch was real. So close.

"Did you ever think about me?" he asked, but then jumped up and began pacing, his movements jerky. "No, don't answer that. It's not fair to ask that without me telling you first. I've thought a lot about you over these last two years. I've never been able to get you out of my head completely and believe me, I've fucking tried."

This was Liz's cue. She should say something. She should tell him that she'd thought about him, too. Far more than she should have. But he wasn't done yet.

"That morning...I was awake. Shit, I know you know I was awake. I wanted to argue with you. I wanted to tell you that we should try. That it was worth it. I regret not saying it. I let you walk out of my life and I've regretted that ever since."

Liz had known that Noah was awake. She'd heard the change in his breathing, but she hadn't said anything to him. It was so painful to leave him. She'd kept telling herself it shouldn't hurt because she barely knew him. It had only been a few hours, but it felt like her heart was being ripped from her chest with someone's bare hands. She'd cried the entire way out of the hotel and in the cab to the airport, all the time feeling like a fool.

Because he hadn't said anything. She'd assumed he hadn't wanted her to know that he was awake. That he didn't want to do the "morning after" thing with her. If he'd pushed that morning, she would have given him her phone number.

"I feel like we're being given a second chance, Libby. I feel like the universe is sending us a message. I don't want to let this pass us by. I've never forgotten you. Did you ever think of me?"

She opened her mouth to reply and then snapped it shut again. She had so much to say and she didn't know how to express any of it. So much had happened since she'd seen him last.

She'd never forgotten him. She'd thought about him often. But she wasn't Libby anymore. She wasn't that person and he didn't know that. She was messed up and had a truckload of emotional baggage, but she couldn't deny the chemistry between them.

Honestly, she'd never felt anything like this with another man. Only him.

And that universe was a crafty son of a bitch, sending her here just when she'd been frustrated and restless with her life. She wanted…more. More than she'd allowed herself in a long time. Noah was more. Her head was telling her to turn away but her heart… It wasn't going to listen and for the second time in her life, she let it run the show.

"I've never forgotten you, either."

Chapter Ten

L IZ DIDN'T HAVE the words to describe the changes she'd been through since she'd last seen Noah.

It wasn't that she hadn't told her story before. She had, multiple times to family and friends. To the police, as well…afterward, although she hadn't known what all she had to look forward to. The trial was the worst. She still had nightmares sometimes about that. Not as much as in the beginning, but every now and then when she was stressed and tired.

"Will you drive me back to Dizzy's house? There's something I want to show you."

It was easier this way. He could see the evidence for himself.

He glanced back at the women sitting on the porch. "Do you need privacy? They can't hear us."

"I know that. No, it's more than that. Please?"

"Of course, I'll take you back. I can imagine that you're exhausted. My family can be overwhelming."

From this moment, honesty had to be the policy.

"Your family is wonderful. It's you that's overwhelming."

His brows shot up and for a moment she could see uncertainty cross his features. She'd expressed herself poorly. She probably would again.

"I mean overwhelming in the best way. Not the worst. The whole situation has me off kilter."

His expression relaxed into a smile. "Me too. But in a good way. Let's go inside and I'll tell Mom and Dad we're going to head out."

"Will they be upset? We can wait until later."

She liked the Andersons and she didn't want to be rude.

"They'll be fine with it. Just give me a minute and then we'll go."

It took almost twenty minutes to actually make their exit, after thanking her hosts and then saying goodbye to everyone there. Mallory gave her a smile of encouragement and the thumbs up sign. It helped knowing that her friend was in support of what Liz was about to do. When they were done, Noah bundled her into his humungous truck and drove toward town.

I'm beginning to get my bearings around here.

"I've never seen a truck this big."

"It is big," Noah agreed with a laugh. "It's for working on the ranch. I have a regular car but I didn't bother with it today. Do you think I'm trying to cover up some feeling of inadequacy by having a big ass truck?"

If he meant penis-inadequacy, then…no. He had no deficiencies there.

"I just never pictured you with a truck like this."

"How did you picture me?"

She could only inwardly roll her eyes at her own stupidity. He was going to think she was an idiot.

"On a horse. You said you worked on a ranch so…"

Now he was laughing harder than before. At least she could say that she was amusing.

"I guess you were picturing the classic cowboy. We do have horses and sometimes we use them, but most of them time we use trucks or ATVs. Do you like to ride? We can do that if you like."

"I've only been once," she admitted. "It hurt to sit down for three days."

His sidelong glance could have steamed up the cab of the truck if she hadn't already rolled down the window to let in the fresh air.

"We don't want you to be sore from…riding. We'll see what we can do."

They'd gone from friendly to hot in less than three seconds. He had a dirty mind and damn, if she didn't as well. She could practically see the filthy images from that night in the hotel that were running through his head. She ought to know. They'd haunted her many of times.

So…that tension was back. It had been gone for a few minutes but the awareness between them had ramped up even higher than before. Every cell in her body was acutely aware of him, sitting only inches away. She couldn't help but study his profile as he concentrated on the road.

He was just as handsome and sexy as she remembered. She'd assumed that she'd built him up in her mind, but no, he was gorgeous. His jaw was firm, his cheekbones impossibly high, and his nose was slightly crooked but it didn't detract from his movie star good looks. If anything, it made him more approachable, more human. Imperfections made art more beautiful, and so it was with Noah as well.

His dark brown hair was slightly longer than before and there were a few curls at the nape of his neck that her hands itched to reach out and touch. She had vivid memories of running her fingers through those silky strands as she rode…

Whoa. Just…whoa. She needed to get ahold of herself. The temperature in the truck had risen about twenty degrees and she almost asked Noah to turn on the air conditioner. What she needed was to *turn off* her libido. Sex had never been that important to her in a relationship but something about this one man had her panting after him.

They had chemistry, an intense physical attraction. Did they have more? They'd talked for hours and she'd genuinely felt an emotional and intellectual connection to him that night, but it was two years later. While their bodies hadn't forgotten did their hearts and heads have a chance of catching up? Was she even capable of a relationship with another human being anymore? If her last boyfriend was allowed to weigh in, the answer would be no. He'd left her in no doubt that it was her, not him that was the problem.

Noah pulled into the driveway next to her own car and killed the engine. Quickly jumping out, he rounded to the passenger side and helped her out the truck. It was a hell of a long way down and falling was a real possibility. She wasn't always the most graceful. Luckily, Noah's strong hands wrapped around her waist and literally lifted her from the seat onto the pavement. He heart fluttered in her chest at his show of chivalry and she chided herself at being impressed in the least.

It's not that big of a deal.

But I liked it.

From habit, she looked over shoulder and then around the perimeter of the home. Mallory had left a light on in the front window and also locked the doors, although she had mentioned that few people in Tremont even bothered with that. Liz couldn't even imagine that. Even in the before of her life, she would have always locked up her house.

Using the key that Mallory had given her, Liz opened the front door and ushered Noah inside, closing and locking the door behind her and then sliding on the chain. If he thought any of her behavior was strange, he didn't say so out loud.

"Would you like something to drink?" she asked as she placed her oversized purse on the coffee table. "We have iced tea, wine, milk, or water."

She and Mallory had made a trip to the grocery store to stock up on essentials. They'd need to go again before the other bridesmaids showed up.

Noah shook his head. "I'd just really like to talk. You said that you wanted to show me something."

The time had come. There was no more delaying the inevitable. She'd known she would tell him the moment he'd opened his front door and stood there like God's gift to women.

She wanted him to understand. Everything. Even the crap that she didn't yet understand about herself. Maybe he could explain it to her.

"You're right. I did say that. Give me a minute. I need to get something from my room."

Slipping into her bedroom, she retrieved the item she needed and then rejoined him in the living room. He'd taken a seat on the couch, which was perfect as she planned to place her display right in front of him on the coffee table. She arranged her items, retrieving the last two from her purse, and then sat down on the cushion next to his.

"This. I wanted you to see this. It surprised Mallory and she asked me about it."

This was her self-defense kit. Pepper spray, stun gun, and handgun. Her friend had been appalled, but Noah didn't appear nearly as bothered.

"What about this is supposed to surprise me? Okay, I think the stun gun is sort of a surprise but a handgun and some pepper spray don't seem like a big deal, especially as you drove here by yourself, but then I'm no stranger to guns. I have a rifle in the truck box and I've been shooting since I was a kid."

Sighing, she reached out and ran a fingertip over the handle of the stun gun. "Would you believe that not long ago I was sort of anti-gun? I didn't want to take guns from people or anything, but I didn't understand why anyone would want to own one unless they were a hunter. I thought people who bought them for self-protection were delusional. I didn't think the world was all that dangerous. What were they scared of?"

Something in Liz's tone must have snagged Noah's attention, because he was gazing intently at the coffee table and then at her. His forehead was furrowed and she could almost see the wheels turning in his head.

"You say that you *didn't* think that the world was dangerous. But you do now?"

Her throat threatened to close up and she had to swallow

hard to keep speaking. "I do."

He didn't reply, leaving the ball in her court. She wasn't sure where to begin so she might as well start where she left him.

"After I left you at the hotel, I got a taxi to the airport. My flight was on time and I was able to make it to the office by early afternoon. The important meeting I needed to attend started at two in our main conference room. I grabbed a soda and made it in plenty of time. There were about five of us in the meeting, and about ten minutes in we heard a scream."

Images from that day, some sharp and others fuzzy crowded her head. Her stomach twisted in her abdomen and the delicious food she'd just consumed at Sunday dinner threatened to make another appearance. She had to pause and take several deep breaths to calm her racing pulse. She could still hear that scream in her nightmares.

"The scream came from one of our newer and younger tellers. She had a gun pointed to her head. That's why she'd screamed."

Liz hadn't allowed herself to look directly at Noah since she'd began speaking, but she couldn't help but take a peek at his expression now.

Troubled mixed with fear. He was afraid of what she was going to say next.

That made two of them.

Placing her shaking hand on her knees to steady them, she went into automatic mode, reciting facts. Facts were easier to deal with. Her emotions were far messier.

"Our bank was being robbed. Three armed gunmen had taken over the bank and wanted all the cash on hand. I'd never been in a bank robbery before, but from what the police told me later is that most of the time they get their money and they leave. They're there as little time as possible. That didn't happen."

She had to pause for a moment to take another breath and swallow the bile that had been creeping up her throat. To his credit, Noah hadn't interrupted but she could feel the tension in his body even a foot away.

"This particular bank robbery team had hit a few banks and gotten away with it. This time, they didn't realize they were being monitored by the police. The cops had somehow figured out where they were going to hit next and they were right on their heels. Shots were fired and it got ugly fast. Everyone they could find were taken as hostages and they herded all of us into the vault area and kept us there at gunpoint. Our lives were threatened several times and we heard them threaten to kill us one by one if their demands weren't met. We were all terrified."

Her voice shook slightly and her legs and hands were trembling. She could still feel the fear that had crawled inside of her that day and had never left, her constant companion.

"And do you know what I thought about while I was sitting there, Noah? It was all I could think about." She turned, their gazes colliding. His normally soft blue eyes a stormy gray. "I kept thinking that if I had just stayed with you in the hotel room that I wouldn't be sitting there. If I had just called in and told my manager I was sick and that I could conference call into the meeting, I could have stayed in that warm bed with you. But I hadn't and it was too late. I was going to die and I was never going to see you again. And you would never know that I regretted my decision."

Noah had his head in his hands, his fingers scraping through his hair. "God, Libby—"

She hadn't been Libby in a long time. She'd tried to put that person completely behind her.

"Please, I need to finish this before I lose my nerve. Unfortunately, my story isn't over. That was really only the beginning."

Her voice was hoarse, like sandpaper and the tears were beginning to burn the backs of her eyes, but she had to keep going. She had to keep her emotions under control. After all this time, she was damn good at pretending that she was fine in front of other people.

He nodded, although it was clear he wanted to speak. He sat back in the cushions of the couch, his shoulders braced as if waiting for a blow to the ribs.

"The standoff went on for several hours, but eventually they gave up and the police came in and arrested them. After I gave the cops my statement, an officer drove me home. He said that I'd been brave, but I didn't believe him."

Restless, she stood and walked over to the window overlooking the front yard. The residential street was quiet, no cars or people in sight.

A cold began to creep over her, chilling her right to the bone. She couldn't take the emotions swirling inside of her so she ruthlessly pushed them away. Not now. Maybe later. It was funny how *later* never seemed to come around.

"You see, I didn't feel brave, and that feeling only got worse as time went on. I went back to work two days later—" She laughed at his incredulity but not because it was funny. It was because her action had been stupid and ill-advised. "Yes, I went back to work right away. The bank was open and I had a job. Most people went back, except that young teller that had screamed. She didn't ever go back. We all thought she was being dramatic but I think she may have been the smartest of us all."

"The bank executives brought in counselors for all us so we could *work through* what had happened. It was clear to me in the first ten minutes of talking to her that she wanted all of us to say that we were fine. So that's what I told her. I think I might have even believed it at the time. Of course, I couldn't have been more wrong."

She heard him move and then he was standing behind her, not touching but she could feel the urgency without him having to say a word. He wanted to comfort her but he didn't want to be pushy, either.

"I promise I'm not going to break down." If anything, she was numb. It was a protective mechanism that she used at times like this and she'd almost perfected it. Until yesterday when she'd seen him in that doorway. It had ripped away at the facade she'd been wearing. Everyone thought she was fine. "Really, I won't. I can't do this unless you give me some space."

There was a noisy exhale, probably from frustration. Well, that made two of them, but then he took several steps back. She could breathe again but she already missed him being close. The scent of his body still hung in the air around her. It was the exact same one he'd used all that time ago and she took a deep lungful, letting the warm aroma fill her with some sense of wellness. She only associated it with the good memories.

"I was pretty good for that first week but then I started not sleeping well, having nightmares, and general anxiety. I became paranoid about the pizza delivery guy. I wasn't sure that woman in the grocery store wasn't casing the joint for a robbery. I didn't like to be out after dark and I really didn't like going to the office. When I was there I was sweaty, jittery, and scared. I couldn't get any work done, of course, and others noticed. I wasn't the only one that was having difficulties. One day I couldn't take it anymore and I walked out. Went home and cried for a couple of hours. Management called and offered me some time off. I didn't take it. Instead, I quit. I knew that I couldn't go back there. They offered to send me to another branch but I was such a mess I turned that down, too."

Noah opened his mouth and then snapped it back shut, but this time she took pity on him.

"What did you want to say?"

"The job in Chicago…"

Ah yes, *that* job.

"I was offered the job a few weeks after my interview but by then I didn't want it anymore. I was in limbo. I couldn't do the job I had anymore and I didn't want to do the job I'd been offered." Mallory turned to stare out the window again, watching the leaves flutter in the breeze. "I guess the bank didn't want me to sue them or something like that, so they offered me a settlement and I took it. It gave me a cushion to figure out what I wanted to do with my life. For about a month I watched a lot of television and stocked up on home security devices like cameras and motion detectors. I took intense self-defense classes and learned to shoot a gun. I vowed that I was never going to be a victim again. And yes, Noah, I saw a therapist. My friends, including Mallory, insisted on it."

Stopping to take a breath, she studied Noah standing only a few feet away. He'd said very little – mostly because she hadn't allowed him to – and she could tell he had about a hundred questions.

"Go ahead," she urged, crossing her arms over her chest as a sort of armor. She could take whatever he tossed out. "You have questions. I'll try and answer them."

"I don't want to interrupt–"

"Yes, you do. Go ahead. I can finish my story later. I'm over the hardest part, actually."

Although whether the story had a lovely happy ending was still up in the air.

"Is that why you're a pottery artist now? Because you quit?"

As questions went, it was a fairly innocuous one.

"It was a suggestion from a friend. It started out as a way to deal with my anxiety and it quickly turned into a career. I'd started pottery in my teens because my stepmother did it and I found it relaxing. For the next month or so I spent almost every waking moment in the studio. She had a friend that had connections in the art world and the next thing I knew I was being offered a chunk of money for what I'd produced. Since I was out of work and the money wasn't going to last forever, I took a leap of faith and started my own business. It allowed me to not have to look for another job because believe me, I was in no shape to do that."

"And it's worked out?"

"I can support myself, if that's what you're asking. I also have enough flexibility that I was able to come to the wedding earlier than everyone else to help Mallory with the last-minute details. So yes…it's worked out."

It had been the one bright spot in all of this darkness.

"And the criminals? They're in jail?"

That question wasn't as easy.

"Yes, they're in jail." She gripped the edge of the windowsill. "I had to testify at their trial."

She shivered as she remembered how the leader of the trio had watched her while she was on the stand. Outwardly he'd looked cool and calm, but there was hate and violence in his eyes. She'd been sitting in the courtroom when the verdict had been read and he'd been led out in handcuffs, as he'd passed by the row she was sitting in, he'd stopped and given her an icy grin before the bailiff urged him forward.

Kenneth Andrew McGuire.

That was his name. Six feet tall, brown hair, light blue eyes, a small scar on his eyebrow, and a tattoo on his forearm of the sun and the moon. She'd had to recite that in court under oath because his lawyer had tried to convince the jury that she had mistaken him for someone else.

If only she could.

Plus, it sure as hell hadn't been anyone else who had surrendered to the cops that day.

McGuire's mother had also come to the trial every single day just as Liz had and she'd sat behind her son, sniffling into a tissue whenever someone said anything negative about him. When Liz had testified, it had been full on waterworks. Liz's therapist had recommended attending the trial saying that she might get *closure* from it. That didn't happen.

"So it's over?" Noah asked. "They're behind bars."

He didn't get it at all. Hadn't he been listening this entire time? Was she speaking a foreign language? She'd just told him she was a mess.

"They're behind bars but that's the thing you don't understand. It's not over, Noah. It may never be over. I'm scared all of the time. Do you know that I check the cameras around my house before I step out of the studio to walk the twenty feet to my back door? Do you know that I sleep with a gun on my bedside table? That's if I actually sleep, of course. Some nights I can't sleep at all. I'm screwed up and I'm not that person that you met that night. Libby is gone and that's why I don't use that name anymore. Because I've changed."

It was simply far too much to ask him to understand. Frankly, no one did.

She was alone for this.

Chapter Eleven

HOLY FUCKING HELL.

Yes, hell. That's what Liz had been through the last two years. He'd had no idea. All this time he'd wondered if she fallen for another man, got married, maybe even had a baby but instead she'd been holding on to sanity with her fingernails.

He remembered waiting in the airport for his flight and that woman pointing out the news on CNN. Hostages at a bank in Denver. He'd never thought...

Never in a million years had he thought it was Liz. If he'd known...

He was pissed, irrationally angry that he hadn't been there to help her through all the shit she'd been thrown. All this time she'd been dealing with this basically on her own.

He hadn't realized he'd made a growling sound until her eyes widened and she'd taken a step back.

"What's wrong?"

It didn't make any sense but he'd say it anyway.

"I'm mad that I wasn't there for you. I wished you had called me or something."

Her expression relaxed and her lips turned up at the corners.

"Called you? How? We didn't even exchange last names, Noah. Whether we did that on purpose or by accident, it didn't change the situation. I didn't have any way to get a hold of you and you didn't have any way to get a hold of me. That was what we decided. We talked about it and we agreed. Neither one of us could have predicted what I walked into that day. Every one tells me it was a fluke, a million to one shot. That I should live a charmed life from now on because the horrible thing has already happened to me."

There was some logic there but he wasn't sure she was free from heartache. However, they might be right about being the victim of a violent crime. She had probably hit her statistical limit.

"Do you believe them?"

Clearly, she didn't if she was packing heat everywhere she went, so it was a stupid question.

"I don't know the odds. I'm guessing if a person gets hit by lightning, they aren't going to play in a thunderstorm because they've already been hit. They'll probably stay inside after that."

He had so many questions, he didn't even know where to go next.

"Are you still seeing a therapist?"

Hopefully she was because it sounded like she had some issues to work on.

Sighing, she shook her head. "You sound like Mallory. My therapist moved to another state and I haven't gotten around to replacing her. I liked her a lot and it's a big pain in the ass to interview new ones. I told her I'd do it when I go home after the wedding."

Noah didn't even want to think about her going home. He'd only just found her again.

"Do you have to hurry back to Denver?"

Liz took a step closer but then hesitated. He wanted to sweep her into his arms and kiss away all of her doubts. He was desperate to show her that he'd never forgotten.

"Are you asking me to stay, Noah? For a second time?"

"Yes."

The answer was simple and straightforward. They'd been given the gift of another chance.

"If I stay and you get to know me, you might end up not liking me anymore."

He couldn't even imagine that scenario.

"It's a possibility," he admitted. "But I have a feeling that it's a remote one. Worst case we realize that what we had won't survive in the real world. Best case…"

His voice trailed off but they both knew what he was saying. They could fall in love. He'd started two years ago and it wouldn't take much to pick up where he'd left off.

"I'm not sure that's the worst case." Her gaze dropped to the floor. "I'm a mess. I know that I have problems. I never feel safe and I don't think that's normal. It sure wasn't how I lived my life in the before. That's how I classify everything now, by the way. The before and the after. You're the before."

He shook his head. "I'm also the after and I'm not scared off, princess. Your problems aren't insurmountable. We can work on helping you feel safe. Together."

"I may be beyond help."

"I don't think so," he replied firmly. "I think you've had a really shitty couple of years but I can see that you don't want to be this way anymore. If you did, you wouldn't be saying that you're a mess. Give me…no, give *us* another chance. Go out on a date with me. You might even have a good time."

She wanted to say yes. He could see it in her eyes. But there was fear there as well.

"I don't want to disappoint you."

"You won't. This is on me. If it doesn't work, then I only have myself to blame since you warned me."

"I suppose a date wouldn't hurt…"

It might even be pleasurable.

✦ ✦ ✦

"WHATEVER YOU'RE DOING, forget about it and let's have some fun."

That pronouncement came from Mallory's smiling lips as she stood in the doorway of Liz's bedroom.

"What?"

"I said let's have some fun. Am I interrupting anything?"

Liz had been checking the security cameras around her home in Denver. She hadn't seen anything except a squirrel running along the back fence, but that hadn't stopped her from staring at the images for the last twenty minutes. Before that she'd checked the windows in her room to make sure they were locked.

Such a social whirlwind. Later, if I'm feeling wild, I might check the windows in the kitchen, too.

She'd warned Noah that she wasn't much fun at parties any-more. He'd stayed for awhile and they'd talked a bit, but then Mallory had come home and he'd politely exited. Before he'd left, however, he'd reminded her about their date tomorrow night.

I have a date with Noah. I never thought that I'd be able to say that.

"Nothing that won't wait. What kind of fun did you have in mind?"

"Does it matter?"

Not really, no. Even if it did, Mallory was the bride so Liz's job was to make sure that she was happy and having the time of her life.

"I'm all yours. What did you have planned?"

There was some giggling from the hallway and then two more heads popped into the doorway – Leanne and Dizzy. Leanne was Carter's cousin and Dizzy was married to Easton, Noah's twin.

"Girl's night," Leann announced, holding up a green bottle with gold foil. "Bubbly champagne, doing each other's hair and nails, and eating ice cream."

Dizzy nodded in agreement. "Definitely champagne. Pink champagne. Are you in?"

It had to be better than what Liz had planned, which was nothing.

"I'm in."

"Pajamas and cocktails," Mallory said with a mile-wide grin. "It's a pajama party. So put yours on and meet us in the living room."

The one thing that hadn't changed from the before in Liz's life was her love for cute pajamas. At home, she had a whole drawer filled with them, some just the pants and others a full set.

For the winter there was flannel and the summer a light cotton, in every conceivable color and pattern. Liz was especially fond of red plaid flannel when it was cold outside.

Tonight she chose a blur jersey pajama pants and paired it with a bright orange t-shirt from hers and Mallory's alma mater. Slipping fuzzy socks on her feet, she also pulled her long hair up and off her face and into a ponytail before scrubbing the makeup off of her face.

When she left her bedroom, she saw that the others had done the same. Leanne was wearing a pink pair of sweatpants with white polka dots and a white t-shirt. Dizzy was wearing purple pajamas with tiny white puppies holding hearts, and Mallory was, of course, the most glamorous one in a pair of red satin pajamas that looked like they'd been made for her. Even her toenail polish matched.

"You're lucky I like you so much."

"Really?" Mallory asked, bracing the champagne bottle on her stomach before opening it. "I do feel lucky but I'm guessing that's not what you were referring to."

"You look amazing. As usual." Liz said it with a dramatic sigh. "Could you take some pity on the rest of us?"

"You look amazing, too." The cork popped and she quickly poured the champagne into a glass to stop the foam from going everywhere. "You all do. In fact, I'd say we were four fine-looking chicks."

"I agree," Dizzy said, her expression solemn. "Tami says the greatest gift you can give yourself is self-acceptance and love."

"Who's Tami?" Liz asked, accepting a flute of bubbling pink liquid.

"My mom. She's full of wisdom, but I would imagine that many mothers have that trait as well. Leann's mom is pretty smart, too."

"She is," Leann agreed. "I swear she can see the future. She's spooky that way. Now how about a toast? Everyone raise your glass to Mallory and Carter. May they live a long and happy life together. And have lots and lots of hot sex."

Mallory giggled and clicked glasses with the other three. "I'll drink to that. I know that Carter would as well."

The bubbles tickled Liz's nose and the cool elixir slid over her tongue and down her throat. Delicious. She loved champagne, although she didn't drink it often except at weddings and New Year's Eve.

Leann sipped at her champagne and then set it on the coffee table. "You know…Dizzy can sort of predict the future, too."

"No, that's not true," Dizzy denied with a shake of her head. "I cannot predict the future."

There was a moment's silence and then Dizzy groaned, rolling her eyes. "Leann thinks that I'm psychic. I'm not, I'm just very intuitive."

"She can tell when a house has spirits," Leann said. "When I was looking to buy a home, I took Dizzy with me. I didn't want to buy anyplace that was haunted."

Mallory shrugged. "I don't believe in ghosts. What about you, Liz? Do you believe in ghosts?"

"I think," Liz replied slowly. "That there is more to this world than what we can see, hear, or touch. I think that I'd like to believe there were ghosts. I'd love to talk to one, someone from the distant past. Wouldn't that be cool?"

Dizzy was nodding but Mallory was shaking her head.

"I don't want to talk to a ghost. That would be…creepy. They're…dead."

"Sort of," Liz agreed. "But they're kind of alive too, because their spirit is still intact. Only their body is dead."

"It seems like you've given this some thought," Mallory observed. "I didn't realize that you believed in hauntings."

Liz had given it some thought. She'd had hours sitting in that bank vault while a gun was pointed to her heart. If that didn't make a person think about life and death, nothing would.

"I'm an enigma wrapped in a riddle and dipped in hot fudge sauce."

The other women laughed at her joke, which was a relief. She could only hope it would serve to help ease the way to change the subject. She wasn't a fan of the topic, to be a hundred percent honest. Mallory knew about Liz's past but the other ladies didn't. Mallory had been through danger herself when she'd been the focus of a serial killer, so she could understand what it meant to fear for her life.

A knock on the door had Leann bounding to her feet. "That's the pizza. I thought we might be a little hungry and want real food in our stomachs before we eat all the chocolate and cheesecake Dizzy made."

"Dizzy's an amazing baker," Mallory said, causing Dizzy to turn a lovely shade of red. "I love everything she makes. Except the rhubarb and strawberry pie, of course. I'm sure it's good but I'm not going to eat it."

Mallory was allergic to strawberries.

"More for the rest of us," Liz said, her stomach gurgling as the aroma of tomatoes and garlic wafted under her nose. She hadn't eaten much earlier because she'd been far too nervous and anxiety-ridden. Now her appetite was reminding her that she liked to eat. "That smells so good."

"Excellent," Leann pronounced. "I was afraid no one would eat because of the upcoming wedding, and the dresses, and all that jazz."

"Are you kidding?" Mallory laughed. "I'm all over this. Should I get some plates or can we eat right out of the boxes?"

It was decided that plates weren't needed but paper napkins were. They ate in silence for the next few minutes, demolishing two medium pizzas. Not bad for women that hadn't even thought they were all that hungry.

Dizzy nibbled on a piece of crust. "We couldn't help but notice that you and Noah went off to the gazebo today. I don't want to be nosy or anything but I think we were all sort of surprised about that."

Liz wasn't quite sure how to respond and Mallory didn't say anything, either. The silence stretched on and Dizzy's gaze whipped back and forth between the two women, her eyes growing round as she realized she'd inadvertently opened a can of worms.

"You know what?" she said loudly, biting her lip. "Forget I asked. Let's talk about something else. What flavor is the wedding cake?"

There was no point in keeping it all a secret. Since she and Noah were going out on a date the next night, they were probably going to find out anyway.

"I met Noah a few years ago during one of his business

trips."

Such a simple sentence but it didn't even begin to cover what all had happened and the myriad of emotions that night evoked to this day.

Dizzy and Leann's mouths formed perfect Os.

"I didn't realize," Leann finally said. "You knew Noah before. Mallory never mentioned anything about that."

"Because she didn't know," Liz explained. "I didn't realize we had a connection through Mallory and Carter, and neither did he until I saw him last night."

"That must have been some surprise," Dizzy observed. "You didn't even have an inkling?"

"Not a one," Liz confirmed. "I'm sure that Mallory said Noah's name at least once but I didn't put it together with the Noah that I'd met two years ago. We didn't know each other's last names, either."

Leann was frowning, and Liz could practically see the wheels turning in her head. Clearly, there was more unsaid about this story than they'd been told.

"You met on a business trip?" she asked.

"In Chicago. I was there interviewing for a job and he was there having some sort of ranch meetings. I'm really not sure what it was all about, to be honest. We both ended up having a drink in the hotel bar and got to talking."

They'd "gotten" to a hell of a lot more but Liz wasn't going to reveal any of those details. From the looks on her new friends' faces it appeared they were working out those details on their own. Smart ladies.

"You never saw him again after that?" Dizzy queried. "And

then you saw him again last night? Wow, that's some major fate action there."

"I never saw him again, and yes, you could say fate was working overtime. It was a shock to see him."

Leann was still frowning. "And you recognized each other? After all that time?"

"It was only two years ago," Mallory defended. "Of course, they recognized one another."

Liz knew what the other woman was trying to say but without saying it out loud.

"We closed the bar down," Liz said. "So we'd spent several hours together."

Her expression cleared, Leann smiled and nodded. "That makes total sense. You two hit it off. But you didn't exchange phone numbers or anything? That's unfortunate."

"It was fine," Liz lied, pushing the pizza box away, her appetite gone. "Who knew that we'd meet up again like this? It was a surprise to us both."

"I think it's a wonderful surprise," Dizzy said with a smile. "The universe always has the last word. You and Noah must have some unfinished business with one another."

That was the understatement of the century.

Chapter Twelve

NOAH WAS HOT, sweaty, and dirty and that was exactly the way he liked it. It was a warmer than usual day and the Montana sun beat down on the back of his neck. He'd spent the morning moving part of the herd from one pasture to another and now he had a few minutes to clean up before lunch.

He didn't have to do the physical work on the ranch any longer. He had plenty of hired hands and he could simply sit in his office all day if he wanted to, but that sounded like hell to him. All of his brothers and cousins spent too much of their time under fluorescent lights taking calls and sitting in meetings. There was no way he could do that. He craved being outdoors even when it was bitterly cold or hotter than Satan's balls. A physical challenge made him feel alive.

It was working the ranch that kept him close to his parents, as well. While they weren't old, they weren't as young as they used to be, either. Being involved in the day to day running of the ranch meant that he saw his mother and father, and his aunt and uncle too, pretty much every day of his life. A few months ago, when his dad had been sneezing and coughing, Noah had convinced him to take a few days rest and recover. When his mother had decided to redecorate the family room, Noah had been there to move the couch this way and then that way. And then back to where it had originally been located in the first place. His dad didn't need to be lugging furniture around anymore. Not when he had healthy sons to do it.

Pulling a handkerchief from his pocket, he mopped at the back of his neck as the sound of ATV engines filled the air. Three of them were heading straight for him, a cloud of dust in their wake. When they stopped a few feet away, Carter, Mallory, and Liz took off their helmets.

This. Right here. This was the woman that he remembered from Chicago two years ago. Liz's eyes were sparkling with happiness and her cheeks were pink with excitement. She looked incredibly excited and not a bit worried about danger lurking in every corner of her world.

Noah helped Liz off of the ATV, tucking her helmet under his arm. "Having fun?"

"That was amazing," she gushed, squeezing Noah's hand. "I loved it."

"I think we've created a monster," Mallory laughed, throwing her arm around Carter. "We've been eating Liz's dust all morning."

"I believe it," Noah said. "Carter drives like our grandmother."

His younger brother flipped him the bird but it was done with a smile. They'd been giving each other a hard time since they were toddlers.

"I didn't realize you were touring the ranch."

Grinning, Carter slapped Noah on the back. "That's my older brother's way of saying that he thinks he knows everything that's going on around here and he's annoyed when he finds out that's not true."

"I'm not annoyed, I'm just surprised."

Because I usually do know what's going around here.

"There's some cold drinks in the barn," Noah said. "Anyone thirsty?"

They all were, of course, so they stomped over to the barn where Noah retrieved four sodas from the refrigerator in the small office. He did most of his paperwork at home but they needed a spot to sign for deliveries and such.

Carter gave Mallory a little nudge with his elbow. "How about a little walk? We can stretch our legs."

Liz smiled in encouragement. "Go ahead. I'm going to rest a bit and cool off."

Noah laughed when the two lovebirds practically ran out of the barn. "I think they wanted to be alone."

"I think they did. Carter isn't too thrilled about Mallory wanting to live separately before the wedding, and frankly, I don't think she's liking it much, either. She told me this morning she hasn't been sleeping well. It could be from wedding nerves or she could be missing him."

Now they were alone. Carter and Mallory wouldn't be back right away and he had unexpected time with Liz. He could already feel that familiar awareness building between them.

"Could be a little of both," Noah agreed, tugging at the collar of his shirt. The office felt hot and stuffy, or maybe it was the way Liz's old blue jeans clung to her delicious curves. She was slimmer than before in Chicago but still absolutely devastating.

"Why don't we give them some couple time? We can relax and you can tell me what you thought of the ranch."

He was surprised by how much he wanted Liz to like it. It would be even better if she loved it. He wanted her to love everything about Tremont and the Andersons.

They settled on the old flowered loveseat in the corner that had once sat in his parents' living room but had been relegated out here when they bought new furniture. *After* all the kids had grown. Now their sofa and chairs were getting a beating from the grandkids.

Damn, she smelled good. Clean and flowery. He, on the other hand, smelled like old socks and was twice as filthy. He tried to back away so she wouldn't get a whiff but the two-cushioned couch was too small and he ended up moving about two inches. They were so close their knees were pressed together and he could feel the heat of her skin through her denims and his own.

Damn. He needed to calm the hell down.

"I think it's huge. As in humongous. I had no idea and I have a feeling I didn't see all of it."

He was sure she hadn't. It would have taken most of the day and some of it was too rugged to travel with an ATV.

"Some of it can only be seen on foot or horseback," he agreed, shifting on the cushion. The pull toward her made it hard to keep his distance. "And in certain times of the year."

"What I saw was quite beautiful. And…efficient. We saw some of your people moving cattle and it was almost like a beautiful synchronized dance. Everyone knew their job and they just did it like it was no big deal. It was fascinating to watch."

Liz couldn't have said anything nicer. It was a terrific compliment. Noah took great pride in the way the ranch was run.

"Thank you. It means a lot that you noticed."

"You're welcome." Her fingers fumbled with the buttons on her jean jacket. He watched fascinated, remembering how those fingers had stroked his skin. "I'm looking forward to tonight."

"Me too."

Christ on a pogo stick, this conversation was painful. It was as if they didn't know each other at all, which was ridiculous. They knew quite a bit, although there was much more to learn.

"I–"

Liz was going to say something but the words stuck in her throat as their gazes clashed. The tension in the room had ratcheted up about a million times and Noah couldn't take it anymore. Without conscious thought, he reached for Liz, tangling his fingers in her hair and pulling her closer until their lips finally met.

Fucking finally.

He'd waited two long years for this and it was even better than he'd ever imagined in his wildest dreams. And he'd dreamed a hell of a lot. She tasted like orange soda and Liz and…more. That was it. He'd figured out her secret.

She tasted like more than he'd ever found with anyone else, anywhere else. Once you have more, you can't settle for less.

Noah couldn't get enough of her heady kisses and she seemed to be of the same mind. Her hands slid over his back, not caring that he was sweaty and dirty and basically rank. He'd forgotten that himself but he couldn't have stopped kissing her to save his life. He drank from those pillowy lips until they both came up for air, gasping for breath, their chests rising and falling rapidly.

"Wow," she mumbled, her amber-colored eyes wide. "That was…"

"Yeah," he agreed. "It was."

"Inevitable," she whispered, her finger tracing his jawline. "It was inevitable."

He had a strange feeling that *they* were inevitable. After all, the universe had done all this work to give them a second chance. He wouldn't screw it up.

Chapter Thirteen

I T WAS THEIR first date, and it was as awkward as Liz's actual first date when she was fifteen and Brian Ryerson had taken her to a football game and then pizza with their friends afterward. They'd kissed on her front porch. No tongue. They'd gone out three more times, kissed some more, with tongue, and then he'd promptly dumped her for Celia Martinson, who had a finished basement with a pool table and air hockey.

It had been Liz's first broken heart.

As nervous as she'd been on that first date didn't hold a candle to how nervous she was tonight with Noah. She'd showered and exfoliated. She'd shaved and moisturized. She'd spent fifteen minutes picking out an eye shadow color and even longer selecting lipstick. Mallory had appeared amused by the entire production but she did say that she'd worried about her first date with Carter. That had been a blind date and of course, it hadn't gone very well. They'd hated each other at first and then the whole stranger dying at the end of the night... They'd had a rough time getting together, to say the least.

But this... was horrible. Their first *real* date was heading to disaster-city and she didn't have a clue how to stop it. Funny how that night so long ago the conversation had flowed so easily but now that the stakes were higher, they sounded like two strangers.

It had happened before. Earlier today when they'd been waiting in the barn for Carter and Mallory, it had been awkward. Luckily, they'd broken the ice by kissing. But now that ice was back along with a hell of a lot of tension. Should she grab him and kiss him again? She wasn't against the idea but there was a hell of a lot more people around now than there were at lunchtime.

Noah had brought her to a local roadhouse for before dinner drinks and to hear his cousin Jason sing. Apparently, Jason was quite good but he only did this every now and then. Since he was in town his friends had convinced him to join up with the band tonight and do a set or two of classic rock. After his cousin performed, Noah had promised to take her to a local Italian eatery where the chicken parmesan was legendary. Mallory had backed up Noah's claim wholeheartedly.

It shouldn't have felt awkward. She and Noah were with a bunch of Anderson couples who had showed up to cheer on Jason. They'd even had to push two tables together so that everyone would have a seat. Mallory and Carter were there, along with Gigi and West, Leann and Zack, Easton and Dizzy, and finally Shane and Arden. Travis and Aubrey were home with a cold. Jason's wife Brinley also joined them, although her husband teasingly threatened to take her onstage as well. Mallory said that Brinley and Jason sounded great together.

There was much joking and bantering going on but Liz could feel the gazes of the others on her as she sat next to Noah.

Did they know the story? The whole story, which included the steamy night she and Noah had spent together? Had he told them that she was a mess and why? She didn't know and she was afraid to ask. Maybe they wouldn't think she was good enough for their brother-slash-cousin. Easton especially was giving her a look that could only be described as *skeptical*. If she had to guess, she imagined that Noah's twin would be rather protective.

Noah pointed toward Liz's half-empty drink. "Another? That looks watered down."

She'd decided against alcohol and had stuck to cranberry juice. "It's fine. Are you getting another?"

He shook his head. "I'm driving. One's my limit."

They'd run out of conversation again. She had the overwhelming urge to kiss him and put an end to all of this nonsense.

He did, in fact, look quite kissable. They were both in casual jeans tonight but not the same ones they'd worn earlier in the day. Noah's were dark indigo and they fit his tight rear end perfectly. He had paired them with a light blue button down and a black pair of cowboy boots. His longish brown hair had been tamed with some product and his jaw and chin were cleanshaven.

I kind of miss the stubble.

"Are you hungry? We can leave right after Jason sings." Noah paused, his gaze darting to the stage where the band was getting ready to play, and then back to her. "Or we can go now. I mean...if you're not having a good time. This might not be your thing."

He didn't say it unkindly. If anything, he sounded panicked

that she might not be having fun. Which she wasn't.

Because she thought that everyone was staring at her.

Paranoid much?

Yes, I am. What's it to you?

Liz didn't want Noah to think that this was about him. This was about her.

"I know this sounds stupid but I feel like everyone is looking at me. Isn't that crazy? I know they aren't but I can't help it."

Noah's brows rose and his smile widened. "Honey, they absolutely are looking at you. In fact, they're looking at both of us."

"Should I even ask why?"

"Because we're the new couple and they're curious. I haven't dated much in the last few years."

He hadn't? That was...interesting. She hadn't, either. One guy for awhile and it hadn't ended well. Then a few blind dates that went terribly. Mallory had urged Liz to go on them based on her own luck but Liz hadn't found her one true love. She had found a guy that didn't trust restaurants and wanted to see his food cooked. They should have gone to those Japanese places where they make your food in front of you on a grill.

That relationship had lasted approximately three hours. Just long enough to go out to dinner, eat, and drive her back home. They'd split the check. No hard feelings.

"It's nice to know I'm not just being paranoid."

Noah threw back his head and laughed, the sound rich and throaty. It sent a tingle down her spine and hitched up that pesky tension between them a few more notches.

He really does look yummy.

"They're just being nosy. It's the downside of being part of a big family."

"Do they know…?"

He shook his head. "I haven't said anything and I don't think Carter and Mallory have."

"Dizzy and Leann know. But they don't…*know* know."

That we had hot sweaty sex in my hotel room. But I think they suspect.

"That's fine. I don't have any big secrets from them. If you want me to, I can make a face at them. They might stop looking. Or they might just try and be more sly about it. It could go either way."

It wasn't important. Now that she knew it wasn't her imagination, it didn't bother her near as much. Surely when the band started up their attention would be elsewhere?

It was only a few minutes later when Jason stepped onto the stage and in front of the microphone. He introduced himself and the guys in the band before launching into a classic rock song from the seventies that Liz was particularly fond of. Two songs later, she could see why the whole family had gathered here tonight. The band was great and Jason could really sing. When they took a short break to check a malfunctioning amplifier, Mallory held up her phone.

"How about a group photo? I'll post it as some pre-wedding fun."

Liz wasn't a big user of social media, but she enjoyed seeing all the pictures that Mallory had posted over the last few months keeping everyone up to date with the wedding planning. Everyone scrunched together to get in the shot, Liz and Noah cheek to cheek.

"Say cheese!" Mallory said in a singsong tone.

They all obediently repeated it, a wide smile on everyone's face. The flash had her blinking but she recovered quickly, watching Mallory tapping on her phone.

"I'm going to post this now while I remember. If I have a few more drinks, I'll forget about it until tomorrow."

Liz leaned over to check out the photo. She wasn't super fond of pictures of herself. She didn't think she was all that photogenic, although she'd been told differently.

Not too bad. I don't have a dopey smile on my face or anything. I've seen worse.

Mallory's fingers hovered over the phone screen. "Do you not like it? I can take another one. Or not post it at all. I thought it was pretty good."

"No, no. It's fine. I was just noticing the lines around my eyes. I guess I'm getting older."

Mallory held the phone closer to her face. "We all are and I don't see what you're seeing. You look great."

"Thanks. We all are getting older, I guess. Life's passing me by so quickly."

Nodding toward Noah, Mallory waggled her brows. "Then don't let it. Go for it."

"That's a definite possibility."

She might have steamer trunk-sized baggage but Noah kept saying that he didn't care.

She wanted to believe him. Badly.

The band came back onstage and their third song was a rock ballad from the eighties.

"May I have this dance?"

Noah was smiling and holding out his hand. She wanted to say yes, her entire body yearning to be as close to his as possible but there was one tiny little problem.

"I don't really know how."

"It's easy. Just follow me. It's a slow song so we don't have to do anything fancy." He leaned over so his lips were close to her ear and she could feel his warm breath on her cheek. "Trust me, honey."

Did she trust him not to let her look like an uncoordinated bear on the dancefloor?

Yes. Yes, she did.

Placing her hand in his, she let him lead her onto the crowd-ed dancefloor. Carter, Mallory, West, and Gigi were out there as well but their attention was firmly on each other.

"Just loop your arms around my neck and stay close."

That was easy enough. Damn pleasurable, too. Her body seemed to fit against his perfectly, although she was five-nine to his six-two. He smelled fantastic and she breathed deeply, filling her lungs with his delicious scent. The room spun for a moment but she was safe as a kitten in his strong arms. For the first time in a long time, she wasn't looking over her shoulder or waiting for something terrible to happen. All was right in her world.

The dance floor was crowded, shoulder to shoulder so they barely moved to the music, their feet shuffling on the wooden plank flooring. Once or twice her toes bumped into his and she started to apologize but he simply shook his head, his lips brushing against her temple.

"Easy, honey. You're doing fine. No worries."

Heat. Her shirt clung to her back as the temperature zoomed between them. Their bodies brushed each other as they moved, his hip pressing against her belly and his thigh between her legs. It was intimate, and close, and sexy, and the arousal for this man and this one alone was beginning to build in her lower abdomen. Like that very first night, she could feel the want inside of her, coiling tighter and tighter until she was sure it would explode any moment.

She'd been playing it safe for a long time, and she longed to be the woman that she used to be. The one that grabbed at life with both hands. Just this once...It couldn't hurt. Right?

"Noah?"

He bent his head, his mouth next to her ear. "Yes, honey?"

"Can we go now?"

He pulled back, obviously surprised by her request. "Of course. Are you not enjoying yourself? Are you hungry?"

Liz was enjoying herself. And she was hungry. For him, specifically.

"Actually, can we have dinner later?"

She couldn't see his expression in the dim lighting but she could see that he nodded in agreement.

"Sure, whatever you want. What do you want to do?"

"Go to your place."

His feet stopped moving and there was silence between them for a long moment.

"My place?"

"Any objections?"

"Fuck, no. Let's go."

Dinner could wait. She'd already waited two years for him. She couldn't wait a minute more.

Chapter Fourteen

B Y THE TIME Noah and Liz arrived at her house that tension between then had built into an electrical storm. She should have kept her hands to herself during the drive, but somehow she couldn't stop herself from trailing her fingers up his muscular thigh or running them over his strong jaw. At one point, he'd groaned and told her that she needed to keep her hands to herself or they were going to end up in an accident.

She'd done it but it hadn't been easy.

After he'd pulled into his garage, he'd quickly rounded the vehicle to open her door and then pull her in for a long, hot kiss. And then another one, and another one. It didn't look like they were going to make it out of his garage and Liz was already searching the building for a horizontal space to have sex.

The hood of the truck. The back of the truck. There was a workbench to the left that might be doable if they moved a few tools. Wait…there was a possibility. A padded weight bench in the corner. A little dusty, perhaps but by far the most comfortable option so far.

"I want you so badly."

Noah's voice was a mere whisper in her ear but in the quiet, out here all alone on the ranch, he might as well have been screaming the words.

She ran her hands down his back straight to his muscled rear end that had been taunting her all night in his well-fitted blue jeans. "I want you, too."

His lips found a spot behind her ear and it almost took her breath away. She had to concentrate to take in oxygen and her knees were beginning to turn to water. So good. Her hands went to his belt buckle but he stopped her, placing his own hands over hers.

"We shouldn't do this out here. We should go inside, where it's comfortable," he panted, his breath warm on her cheek.

Frankly, Liz didn't give a shit if they did it in a bed. It had been two long years and that pent-up longing had broken free. She'd take Noah any way she could get him. But she did as he asked, letting her hands fall to her sides.

"I don't think I can wait," she said, taking a deep breath, her heart slamming against her ribs. Her gaze couldn't help but see the hard ridge of his arousal outlined by his jeans.

"I want to slam you up against the side of my truck and have my wicked way with you," he said with a groan. "But that would be wrong."

That sounded like heaven to Liz. What was the problem?

"Why would it be wrong?" she blurted, keeping her gaze trained on his face instead of his crotch.

He frowned as if he didn't understand that question. "Be-cause...it would be disrespectful."

Noah was a sweet man but he didn't have a clue. Didn't he see how hot and bothered she was? Both of them were breathing like they'd just finished a marathon.

Hooking her finger in his waistband just as she had that night long ago in the hotel, she pulled him closer so that she could feel his hard cock up against her belly. A pleasurable shiver ran up her spine at the sensation.

"You respect me just fine. What I need is you inside of me, Noah, preferably as soon as possible. I don't want to wait. We can make love in a bed later tonight."

He appeared truly conflicted at her words. She could feel how much he wanted her but...

Pulling his head down, she pressed her lips against his, the kiss sizzling hot with desire. When she eventually pulled away, she had to gasp for breath. "I know you want it to be special. I do, too. But don't you understand it will be no matter what? Because we're together."

Whatever she'd said seemed to work. He stepped back and began working on his belt buckle, a huge grin on his too-handsome face. There really ought to be a law against being that good-looking. All the Andersons – male and female – had won the gene pool lottery.

His pants unbuttoned, he began working on her jeans, his fingers awkward in their haste. He buried his face in her neck, licking and nipping at the skin and sending sparks straight to her lower abdomen, her arousal building quickly. She tugged at his shirt, a few buttons popping off and skittering away probably never to be found again, but she'd successfully bared his chest to her questing hands. Rubbing her palms against his warm flesh, she felt him shudder against her.

While she'd opened his shirt, he'd managed to slide her blue jeans and panties down her legs, taking her shoes with them so she was naked from the waist down. The temperature in the garage should have made Liz feel chilled but instead it felt like a sauna. Her skin was shiny and damp as Noah placed open-mouthed kisses on her thighs and belly. Arrows of arousal shot straight to her clit and she moved restlessly under him, her need growing out of control. She was more than ready for him now.

Her fingers dug into his wide shoulders and she hooked one of her legs around his lean hips. "Now, Noah."

Digging into his back pocket for his wallet, he pulled out a foil square. The same brand he'd used that night two years ago. Funny how her brain had locked onto even the smallest details.

The mole on his chest, just above the left nipple.

A small round scar on his left cheek. So faint she'd had to look closely.

The ring of gold right around his pupil that could turn dark when he was close to his climax.

His long, lush lashes so dusky against his skin when he closed his eyes.

Liz slid her hands down, tracing his ridged abs with her fingertips. He'd told that he did physical work on the ranch, even though he didn't really have to, and it clearly showed. Every spot on his body that she touched was firm and muscled, not an ounce of spare flesh to be found.

While she'd been fantasizing, Noah had ripped open the foil packet with his teeth. Not wanting to be left out, Liz helped him roll it on, giggling like teenagers at their haste.

Noah held up one finger before swinging up into the extended cab of the truck. "One second, babe. Let's try and get a little comfortable."

Reaching down, he lifted her easily off of the floor and placed her on the seats if she was made of the finest crystal. She scooted back on the buttery soft leather, and he came down on top of her, his cock nudging at her entrance.

"Are you ready for me?"

Was he kidding?

"About ten minutes ago. Fuck me, Noah."

He didn't make her wait any longer, pressing forward until he was deep inside, rubbing against her sweet spot and sending a jolt of electricity to her toes and fingertips. It took a few thrusts to find their rhythm but when they did, he rode her hard and fast as she urged him on, whispering filthy suggestions into his ear as they climbed the hill in unison.

Flames licked at her flesh as she teetered on the precipice, so close to going over. With each stroke, Noah's groin rubbed against her clit and it would only take one...two...three...

Liz screamed his name as her orgasm hit, her body bowing off of the seat, her toes curling as pleasure ran through her like a waterfall. Noah's climax came right after hers, his head thrown back and his jaw tight.

When it was over Noah lay on top of her, their breathing ragged and labored, their skin damp. Running her fingers through his silky hair, she pressed small kisses to his jaw.

"That was really great but I kinda can't breathe down here."

She giggled and he tickled her ribs, drawing even more laughter from her. Levering up, Noah sat back on his haunches and looked down at her with a wicked grin. She could only imagine the sight she made, naked from the waist down, hair a rat's nest, and shiny makeup. He, however, didn't seem to mind how she looked. There was that warmth in his eyes that she was beginning to really, really like.

"It's your own fault, woman. You wore me out. I'm not as young as I used to be."

"You sound like you're eighty," she teased. "You seem pretty spry for an old man."

Waggling his eyebrows, he bent down and pressed a kiss to her abdomen, setting off a new set of quivering. She'd never get enough of this man.

"Let's go inside and you'll see just how spry I can be."

She couldn't say no to that. In fact, she couldn't imagine ever saying no to him.

She was that far gone.

Chapter Fifteen

NOAH STOOD BAREFOOT in his kitchen wearing nothing but a pair of sweatpants. And a smile.

A huge motherfucking grin, if he was being completely honest.

Making love to Liz had been miraculous, almost life changing, although that might be taking things a bit too far. Since that first time, he'd assumed that he'd blown their night together out of proportion, made it better than it was, but no. It was just as amazing.

He loved that she wasn't afraid to come out and tell him what she wanted. Namely…him.

They'd practically raced out of the roadhouse and back to his place, pulling off their clothes because they were in the way. It had been hot, raunchy, and fucking fantastic.

He was never selling that truck. Thank goodness, he'd bought the biggest damn one on the car lot that day. Afterward, he'd loaned Liz a t-shirt to wear and they'd headed into the kitchen, their stomachs growling, to find something to eat.

"Do you like steak?" he asked, his head in the refrigerator. Liz was perched on a bar stool at the island. "It's not chicken parmesan but I can make twice baked potatoes to go with it."

"With cheese?"

"Fuck, yes. Sour cream, too."

"I'm totally on board with that. It sounds delicious. Can I help?"

"I've got this. You just sit there and look beautiful."

He must have said something funny because she was laughing, her hand on her stomach and her head thrown back. Her chocolate brown hair was tousled around her shoulders, her smooth golden thighs bare. She looked so damn sexy he almost dragged her back in the bedroom and had his way with her again.

Down, boy. Feed her first.

"I'm only eye candy to you?" Liz stuck out her lower lip in a pout. "How disappointing."

Scrubbing the potatoes clean, he gave her a nudge with his elbow. "You're a hell of a lot more than that."

She was beginning to become everything. It should have terrified him but instead he was happy. He was ready for it. He'd come to the point in his life where he was more than willing to make the compromises and sacrifices of a serious relationship.

When she looked at him, he could see the emotion in her eyes. She wasn't unaffected. She felt it, too. He wasn't out there on a limb all by himself.

"You're not so bad yourself."

Her words were soft but he easily heard them.

"So tell me about this pottery business you have going. I want to know everything."

Noah had placed a bag of cheese on the island and Liz

pinched a bit and popped it in her mouth. "I told you most of it. I started it as therapy but it quickly became my full-time job which is good because I needed a way to support myself. I couldn't go back to the bank and I really didn't want the whole corporate gig anymore. I'm not rich by any stretch of the imagination, but I do okay as long as I don't go on extravagant vacations and buy expensive shoes. That was sort of tough…giving up my shoe habit, but now I get to wear comfortable clothes all day so it's a tradeoff I can live with."

"My mother said that you do functional pottery."

"I do," she confirmed, pushing a stray strand of hair off of her cheek. "Most of what I create can be used. I do also make some art pieces but that's not my bread and butter, so to speak. Most people want to use what they buy."

"What's your biggest seller?"

"Vases," she replied promptly, stealing another pinch of cheese. "Followed by bowls and then tea seats."

"If you eat all of the cheese, there won't be any for the potatoes."

"It was only two teeny-tiny little bites, barely big enough for a mouse."

She was absolutely adorable sitting there in his t-shirt sneaking shredded cheese. He leaned down and dropped a kiss on her cute as pie nose.

"You're the sexiest mouse I've ever had in my home."

Giggling, she shook her head. "What is it about men and their clothes on women? I wouldn't think you were so cute if you threw on one of my nightgowns, or maybe a pair of yoga pants and a tank top."

His shoulders shook with laughter. "I can see why. My chest hair alone would clash with a cute little nightie. Luckily for you, I don't want to wear your clothes. As for women in men's clothes, I don't know why we like it but we do. There's something extremely primal about you wearing my shirt."

She gave him that look. *That* one.

"Turns you on?" Her voice had dropped a few octaves. At this rate, they might never get to eat dinner.

"It does, but I'm trying to ignore it because both our stomachs are growling like hungry lions. We need to eat to keep our strength up."

She stuck out her lower lip. "You're right, but that doesn't mean I'm happy about it. Now are you sure I can't help?"

"I've got it all under control. I want to keep asking you questions about your pottery and your life now. Is that okay?"

"It is. Fire away. Get it? Fire away? It's a pottery joke."

Liz was literally cracking up at her own bad joke, and she had Noah laughing, too. He hadn't had this much fun with a woman since…the last time they'd been together.

He finished broiling the steaks and making the potatoes. They sat down at his rarely used kitchen table to eat. Everything tasted delicious, if he did say so himself, or maybe it was simply the company that made normal, everyday food taste gourmet. Both of them finished every bite of their meal, patting their stomachs when they were finished.

"I am so full," Liz groaned. "But it was so good I couldn't stop eating. Potatoes and cheese are a match made in heaven. You're a good cook."

"Mom taught all of us, but I wouldn't say that I have a large repertoire. I can make steak and potatoes, hamburgers and hot dogs on the grill, and roast chicken. Oh, and I also make a mean breakfast. Pancakes, eggs, bacon, toast. If you stick around until morning, you'll see for yourself."

The ball was in her court. He'd take her back to Dizzy's later if that's what she wanted, but he'd kind of hoped she'd want to stay here.

"I'd love to have you cook breakfast for me but…"

That hope was fading fast.

"But?" he prompted. "You're worried I snore?"

She shook her head and reached across the table, placing on of her small hands on top of his larger one. Her skin was pale and delicate in comparison to his tanned and work-roughened hands.

"I know you don't snore. It was just thinking that as much as I'd like to stay here with you tonight, it might be rude to leave Mallory on her own at Dizzy's. I'm supposed to be the maid of honor, remember? It's not very honorable to leave the bride because the sex is out of this world."

Clearing his throat, Noah stroked his chin. "Sorry, I didn't hear anything but that the sex is out of this world. Did you say anything else?"

Liz rolled her eyes. "You are such a goofball."

"Guilty as charged. You make a good point, though," he conceded. "You are supposed to be here for Mallory and it would probably be rude to leave her on her own at the house tonight. I know she didn't mind about this evening because she and Carter are spending it together, but I don't want to hog all of your time. I guess I'll have to take you back to Dizzy's later."

Liz stared down at her hands. "With the other ladies coming into town tomorrow morning, I'm going to be very busy until after the wedding."

He'd been thinking about that.

"I've been thinking about that too, Liz. I'll build you a pottery studio with my own two hands if you'll stay on after the wedding for awhile."

She looked up and he could see tears sparkling in her eyes. He wanted to reach out and tell her it was all going to be okay but he didn't know that for sure. They were both flying blind here, hoping for the best.

"How long is awhile?"

He wanted to say forever but it was too soon for that. As skittish as she was, he didn't want to scare her to death.

"I know you have a life back in Denver," he replied carefully. He needed to use the right wording here. They'd come to an important juncture. "And I respect that. But I'm hoping that you will give us a chance. A real chance. We didn't want to do long distance before, but of course now we know that the connection between us is the kind that isn't going to fade away easily. I'd be willing to do long distance with you but I was hoping that you might stick around here in the beginning. If you can't do that then I'd talk to my family and possibly take a leave of absence. Come visit you."

Her eyes went wide. "You'd come with me to Denver? For real?"

She wasn't getting it. She was that important. He wasn't about to let her slip through his fingers again.

"I would. It wouldn't be easy as there's always work to do

around this place, but I want us to have the best chance."

She didn't answer right away, as if digesting his reply.

"What do you know about pottery studios?"

"Not a thing," he answered promptly. "You'd have to tell me what you need, but I promise you I'd build the best damn pottery studio this side of the Mississippi if it would mean that you'd spend more time here. I can put in right in the backyard with electricity and running water. I can get started the day after the wedding. The family owns a construction business if I can't handle it myself."

"It might be a bigger job than you imagine," she warned. "There's more to it than you would think."

"I'm not afraid of a little hard work." Noah's throat was tight with emotion. He wasn't going to beat around the bush or play games. This was far too important. "What I'm afraid of is losing you again. I can't let that happen."

She was already shaking her head before he finished. "It wouldn't happen because I wouldn't let it happen."

His fingers laced with hers. "I'm glad to hear that. You're the first person I've met that made me want to make compromises."

A few tears slid down her creamy cheeks. "I want to make compromises for you, too."

"Then let's do it," he urged, his heart slamming against his ribs. "We have time before I have to take you back to Dizzy's. Let's make a plan for how we're going to do this. Let's make promises we intend to keep."

This was their second chance.

✦ ✦ ✦

"KENNETH MCGUIRE IS dead."

Noah was sitting in his cousin Jason's kitchen the next morning. He'd asked Jason to check into the bank robbery in case there were important details that Liz was leaving out. He couldn't help her over her fears if she wasn't honest with him.

He hadn't, however, expected this news.

"He's dead?"

"Dead," Jason confirmed, refilling his own coffee cup and then Noah's. "Two months ago. He was in a fight with another inmate and was stabbed. The other guy was pretty messed up as well, but he pulled through apparently and was immediately transferred to another prison in case any of McGuire's friends wanted revenge."

"Why didn't anyone tell Liz?"

Jason shrugged. "Prosecutors move on. Staff changes. Whoever is in charge now probably didn't tell anybody. It might have been in the local papers, especially if there was a slow news day. It's sad to say, but if he'd been paroled from prison they might not have told her. Did McGuire make threats against her?"

"No, but Liz said that he gave her a look when he was led out after sentencing. I know that sounds vague, but she said that he grinned at her and it wasn't because he was happy about the outcome. He specifically did it to shake her up. He singled her out and she wasn't the only one to testify."

"She wasn't. I have a transcript of the trial, if you're interested. I'm guessing he singled her out because she's extremely attractive. She also did a hell of a job on the stand. I didn't have time to read the whole transcript but I did read through her testimony. She was poised and well-prepared. Kept her cool and answered the questions directly and simply. He was going to be found guilty anyway, but she certainly did the job the prosecution asked of her."

"I do want to see the transcript," Noah decided. "I want to be able to help Liz through this and I think I'll be better equipped if I know the case details well."

Jason reached over and retrieved a thumb drive from the counter. "It's all here, but I warn you some of the details are stomach-queasy stuff. I've heard and seen much worse but you're a civilian."

Noah accepted it, tucking it in the front pocket of his jeans. "I'd like to think that I can take it, cousin. Is it grisly? Because according to Liz no one was killed."

"They weren't, but McGuire and his crew knocked around the security guard and a few other of the males in the group. Mostly it was a case of psychological terror for the hostages. They were threatened with death several times and they never knew whether they were going to live or die until the thieves were in custody. I did a little checking and Liz wasn't the only one with trauma. I don't know if she knows this, but pretty much every one of the employees in that branch have either quit or been transferred out of state in the last two years. At their request. She was just one of the first."

Noah doubted Liz knew any of that because by her own omission she'd kept her distance from her former co-workers. It might help her to know that she wasn't the only one as she'd made it sound when she'd told him the story.

"Is there anything else I need to know about that robbery?"

"I don't think so," Jason replied, sipping his coffee.

"McGuire was a career criminal who had moved up from knocking over liquor stores and gas stations to robbing banks over the years. He'd done time before and even if he hadn't been caught that day, he was going to do time again. From what I could see in his file he wasn't interested in rehabilitation. His brother and father were the same. Both career criminals. You could say that robbery was the family business."

If only Liz had stayed with Noah that day in Chicago.

"Did you say something?" Jason asked, his brows pulled together. "I didn't hear you."

"I said that she wouldn't have been there if she'd stayed with me in Chicago. That's where I met her. I was on a business trip there and we were staying in the same hotel."

Jason gave him a shrewd look, almost as if he could tell that Noah was leaving out some damn important details. Important, but private.

"I see. I kind of understood that you knew her from sometime in the past but I wasn't sure how."

"You can tell the family, if you want. It's not a secret."

"It's not mine to tell."

"As I said, it's not a secret. We hit it off in Chicago and I asked her to stay another day so we could spend more time together. She said she had to hurry back to Denver for a meeting at work. So she went back and they were robbed the same day. I didn't know any of that happened until I saw her again a few days ago."

Jason looked like he had a bunch more questions but to his credit he didn't ask any of them.

"It's good that you two ran into each other again. You look

almost happy. The family was getting worried about you."

"Were you worried?"

Jason chuckled and shook his head. "Fuck, no. I knew you'd be fine. You're an Anderson. We're survivors."

So was Liz. Maybe that's why she and Noah were so good together.

Chapter Sixteen

THE OTHER TWO maids of honor showed up mid-morning, wearing huge smiles and ready to have some fun. Celia was tall and blonde, quite athletic and incredibly smart. She was currently a researcher at a biomedical firm. Dani was petite and curvy, with the most gorgeous thick and lustrous auburn hair. Her family owned a small independent cosmetics company and she was now the CFO.

Liz couldn't help but be amazed by how they'd all managed to stay friends. There had been a myriad of boyfriends, engagements, marriages, a few kids, several jobs, a cancer scare, and of course Liz's own encounter with violent crime. For all of it, they'd been there for each other far more than their own families. They were like sisters. And for the first time in over a year they were all in the same room. Dizzy's living room, to be exact.

They'd ordered barbecue takeout for lunch and everyone was sitting around the coffee table, eating and talking at the same time, catching up about how awful air travel was and how amazing the upcoming wedding was going to be. Celia showed off pictures of her two kids that she'd taken right before getting dropped off at the airport. Dani showed off pictures of her animals, two adorable dogs and a sweet little cat. Her husband was taking care of them and was also planning to plant some flowers in the front yard while she was gone. She'd chosen red begonias.

There was the usual moaning and groaning about jobs and politics, bad drivers and demanding in-laws, but for the most part the conversation was upbeat. They were together and that was far more important than any petty complaints they might have.

"Thank you so much for letting us choose our own dresses," Celia said. "I was in my brother's wedding a few months ago and I swear the dresses were so ugly all the guests needed dark glasses just to look at them."

"How bad were they?" Mallory asked. "On a scale of one to butt ugly?"

"A thousand," Celia pronounced with a grin. "My sister-in-law's colors were pale yellow and pale blue but somehow the dresses were almost neon. I swear they glowed in the dark. I looked like a giant neon banana. I was at least six inches taller than the other bridesmaids, too. The wedding photos are hilarious. I really like her though, and she seemed happy. That's all that's important."

Dani coughed delicately into her paper napkin. "My three siblings have all married and I haven't been in one wedding party. Believe me, I'm not complaining in the least about it, either. I think that my resting bitch face discourages them from asking me. That, and my total disdain for the modern wedding industry that encourages young couples to go into tens of thousands of dollars in debt."

Dani and her husband Charlie had been married on the beach in Hawaii, wearing bathing suits and leis. Just the two of them and the officiant. She'd invited all her friends to a fantastic party about a month later.

"Then I feel very special that you agreed to be in my wedding," Mallory said. "Very special, indeed."

Dani lifted her glass toward her friend. "Your wedding is different and I'm happy to be in it. You're not doing all that garter and bouquet stuff. So sexist, but they wrap it up as *tradition*. Shit, families used to sell brides. That was a tradition, too. Doesn't mean that we should keep doing it."

Celia leaned back against the bottom of the couch. "So now that Mallory is getting married that just leaves our Liz, who I believe after Dani's wedding reception said that she couldn't see herself getting married for at least ten more years. That was five years ago."

Did I really say that? It kind of does sound like me.

"I stand by my statement. I'm in no hurry to tie the knot."

Dani frowned. "Are we such a bad example of marital bliss that we're scaring you away?"

Liz laughed and shook her head. "Not in the least. I'm just not in any hurry, that's all. Marriage has never been all that important to me."

"It wasn't to me either until I met Charlie," Dani pointed out. "I truly didn't care about getting married but once I met him it didn't seem like such a terrible idea anymore. Not that I think that everyone should get married. I don't. Frankly, I was surprised by my own reaction."

They'd all been surprised.

"Liz might be closer to marriage than she thinks."

That remark was from Mallory who was grinning like a loon. No one had ever accused her of being subtle with her friends.

Celia's brows rose. "Is there a man in the picture? Spill all the details. Us old married women live vicariously through the single friends in our life, so have some mercy."

Liz gave Mallory a mean look. "I would have said something eventually. I'm sort of seeing Carter's older brother Noah. It turns out we'd met before in Chicago a few years ago."

Dani sucked in a breath, her eyes round. "Are you talking about *the* Chicago guy? Him?"

Liz had told Dani about Noah. It had been a tear-filled night a few months after the bank robbery. She hadn't been able to get any sleep because she kept checking the doors and windows and pacing the floors. In desperation, she'd called Dani who was a notorious night owl, hoping she'd be awake. The entire story had tumbled out of her, including a few salacious details about the night she and Noah had shared together. She'd been blaming herself for not staying with him, saying over and over that she'd made a huge mistake.

Dani, of course, had calmly and rationally talked her down and had made everything seem a hell of a lot better than it had looked mere hours before. She was good like that. She had a great voice, almost hypnotic and before she knew it, Liz had stopped crying and had actually slept a couple of hours that night.

Mallory's mouth hung open. "Wait...you knew about Noah? How come I didn't know? Celia, did you know?"

The other friend shook her head, her gaze darting around

their circle. "I didn't know. I mean, I kind of knew. Liz had said she'd met a guy that she really liked but it didn't work out. I just didn't know his name or that it was on her trip to Chicago."

Shit, this was going sideways quick.

"I told Dani during a panicked middle of the night phone call when I was crying and couldn't sleep. I was not purposefully keeping any of this from you. Honestly, the whole thing with Noah was completely eclipsed by the robbery. The only reason I told her was because I was regretting not staying another day in Chicago like he asked me to."

Mallory nodded. "I can imagine you would have a hell of a lot of second-guessing yourself. I did that, too. If I hadn't gone on that date. If I hadn't gone to the bathroom. All that stuff."

"It doesn't help much, though," Liz admitted. "Eventually I had to tell myself that I couldn't think about him, if only for my own sanity."

"But you didn't stop thinking about him, did you?" Celia queried softly.

"I didn't, and from what he says, he didn't either."

"That's so romantic," breathed Celia, a dreamy smile on her face. "It's like it was meant to be. Fate and the universe working together to give you and Noah a second chance."

It was romantic. It was also sort of scary. Liz didn't want to mess this up.

Dani took a sip of her soda and then placed the can on the coffee table. "How are you doing these days?"

Celia scowled at her friend. "That's a shitty question."

Dani sat up, her chin lifted. "How is it shitty? I asked a straightforward question. It's not like we have a bunch of secrets between us. We're all friends here and no one is going to judge the other. I asked Liz how she's doing. If she doesn't want to answer me–"

"It's fine," Liz interrupted, not wanting any disagreements between them. They were supposed to be having fun and enjoying being together. "It's absolutely fine. I'm doing okay. Not fantastic, but okay. I'm here, aren't I? A year ago, I wouldn't have attempted the drive all by myself but I did it."

From the expression Mallory was wearing, Liz could tell that she was thinking about the gun.

"I do still carry a concealed weapon," Liz went on to say. "For good or bad, it makes me feel safer."

Dani's lip curled in contempt. "Frankly, I don't blame you one bit. The world can be a dangerous place and you were making the trip from Denver all alone. Criminals and evil exist in this world. Do you remember the look on McGuire's face during the trial? So disdainful. He even tried to pretend that he was innocent and he was tricked into doing it by his friends."

Celia wrinkled her nose. "He should have done what the others did—plead guilty for a lighter sentence. Arrogant shit."

"Are they all still in prison?" Mallory asked. "They haven't gotten out for good behavior or shit like that?"

"Last I heard they were still there and going to be for a long, long time. They used firearms during the commission of a crime and they made their sentences worse."

Dani frowned. "You don't know if they're there?"

Liz rubbed at her temples where a headache was beginning to bloom. She needed another glass of wine. "My therapist said that it wasn't healthy to fixate on them. That I needed to focus on myself and feeling more comfortable in the world."

Celia pursed her lips and then blew out a breath. "I can see where they were coming from there. She wanted you to feel safe whether they were behind bars or not. Their incarceration shouldn't affect you one way or the other."

"I've thought about leaving Denver," Liz confessed. These were her best friends, after all, and she didn't have any secrets from them. "I thought I might get a fresh start in a new place. But then I thought that it might be wimpy to leave, like I wasn't facing up to it."

"You could come here," Mallory replied eagerly. "Tremont is a lovely place to live."

Celia was nodding in agreement but Dani appeared conflicted. She didn't like spur of the moment decisions, preferring to weigh all the options first. It made her a hell of a CFO but it drove her friends a little bonkers.

Sighing, Mallory nudged Dani with her elbow. "Spill it. Clearly you have issues with what I just said."

Dani shrugged. "It's just...I think that Liz has a point. Would she be running away instead of facing her fears? I don't have the answer to that one but I think it's worth delving into. Your problems just follow you and you end up dealing with them anyway."

"I'm trying to deal with them," Liz said. "I'm not trying to run from them, but Denver won't ever be the same for me after what happened."

Celia leaned forward, wrapping her arms around her knees. "Do you feel safer here?"

Yes, but...

"I do but probably not for the reasons that you think. I feel safer because I have my friends all around me."

"What about your friends in Denver?" Mallory asked.

Good question. Tough answer. What friends?

"Most of my friends were from when I worked at the bank. When I left…"

"You didn't exactly take them with you," Celia finished for her. "It makes sense, though."

"Honestly, I don't think they wanted to be around me any more than I wanted to be around them. We all reminded each other of that traumatic event. We sort of drifted apart. I have nice neighbors but I wouldn't call them close friends. We're more wave when we drive by or chat over the mailbox kind of acquaintances."

"That's just awful." Dani's eyes glittered with unshed tears. "Why didn't you tell us? We would have visited more often or brought you to see us. We thought you had lots of friends there to support you."

I didn't want to dump my problems on other people.

"It wasn't terrible, actually. You all took turns staying with me in the weeks afterward, and then later I needed some time to myself to process it all. Because of all of you, I never once felt alone. You were always a phone call away. We texted regularly and we had our weekly Skype call. And we did visit each other. I didn't need you to be physically in the room with me, and you all had your own lives, too. You dropped everything to come to my aid and I'm so grateful for that, but I needed to stand on my own two feet. And I did."

"You certainly have," Mallory agreed fervently. "We're all

incredibly proud of you. I hope you know that."

Celia and Dani were both nodding vigorously in agreement.

"I'm proud of me too, but I still have a ways to go."

"The fact that you're thinking about the future is a huge step forward," Mallory insisted. "Thinking about moving, starting to date Noah. That's real progress."

Liz quirked an eyebrow. "Even if I'm packing heat while I do it?"

"Even then. This second chance with Noah could be the start of something wonderful. You never know," Mallory giggled. "These Anderson boys can be mighty addicting. Next thing you know, you're in love with one of them."

Liz had a feeling that she could fall in love with Noah quite easily. She'd already fallen for the man that she'd met before. If he was anything like it in the after…

She was toast.

Chapter Seventeen

NOW THAT THE other bridesmaids had arrived in Tremont, it wasn't as easy for Noah to get time with Liz. The ladies were busy with last-minute dress fittings, wedding favor craft sessions, and just generally catching up after not seeing one another for months. He hadn't seen her at all yesterday but she'd managed to carve out a few hours the next afternoon while her friends rested and caught up with their loved ones back home.

He'd picked her up from Dizzy's house and taken her to the diner for a late lunch. They were both hungry and it was cheeseburgers and fries all around. He didn't bring up the subject of Kenneth McGuire until the waitress had disappeared back into the kitchen after taking their order.

He reached across the table and laid his hand over hers, still marveling at how satiny soft her skin felt. "I'm glad I could see you today."

"I'm glad I could see you, too."

There was a warmth in those amber eyes that he recognized. She was thinking about the other night and honestly, so was he. He'd thought of little else but her, and he wasn't unhappy about that in the least.

"I have some news for you that you might find surprising."

"Okay…I'm listening."

He'd thought about how to give her the news and there were about a dozen different options, but the most straightforward seemed the best way. Might as well start off with the biggest news.

"Kenneth McGuire is dead."

Liz blinked once, then twice, then shook her head. "What? He's… I mean…how?"

"Prison fight. He's gone, Liz."

Sitting back, she stared out of the window of the diner for a long time. Noah kept quiet, letting her gather her thoughts together. This had to have come as a shock.

"He'd dead."

Her words were barely audible. She was still looking away, her attention somewhere else. Possibly the past?

Eventually she turned her gaze back to him, her expression stormy. "He's dead? From a fight? When? And how do you even know this?"

"I asked my cousin Jason to look into what happened at the bank. He found out that McGuire is dead. He died a couple of months ago."

Liz pressed her lips together and she pulled her hand back, placing it in her lap.

"You did what? You…checked up on me?"

Shit. She didn't understand. He needed to right this ship immediately before it hit an iceberg.

"No, not at all. I just wanted to be able to help you as much as possible and I needed to know if there were any details about the robbery that you'd left out."

When he said it out loud...it didn't sound any better. In fact, it kind of sounded worse.

Fuck. Danger. Red alert.

"I was just trying to make sure that I could help you, Liz. I'm sorry if I've overstepped any boundaries."

Steepling her fingers, she took her time responding while Noah sweated it out.

"You did cross a boundary. A big one. You went behind my back because you didn't trust that I told you the truth."

Her words were calm and controlled, but her cheeks were red. She was pissed off and Noah didn't blame her. In his zeal to help and protect, he'd fucked up. Royally.

"*Mea culpa.* I messed up big time. I didn't think it through. I just wanted–"

Liz held up her hand and shook her head. "No, you don't get to mitigate it, Noah. You were about to say that you wanted to help me. You made this situation about what *you* wanted, not about what I wanted. Your wants are not more important than mine. They're equal. If you were concerned that there was something you didn't know, you should have come to me. If you'd told me that you wanted your cousin to check into the robbery, I would have told you to go ahead but that I'd told you what I considered to be the most important details. But you went behind my back. I have to wonder if that's because you felt, deep down, that it was wrong."

He was in deep shit. Far deeper than he'd originally thought.

Think. Don't be a jerk. Think before you speak.

"You're absolutely right," he replied slowly, taking a deep

calming breath. Was this their first fight? Shit. He didn't want his stupidity to ruin what they had between them. "My wants are not more important than yours. I should have discussed it with you. I guess it's in my nature to step up and try and take control of a situation. It's what I have to do in my job every day, but clearly, this was the wrong call here. I really am very sorry."

The red color in her cheeks was gone and she didn't appear as agitated. "Thank you for apologizing. As long as you understand that going forward, I'm not a situation to manage or control. I get that you need to be that way in your job. That makes sense. But I'm not the ranch, I'm a human being. If we're going to do this, we have to be equal partners."

"I want to do this. I am sorry."

Blowing out a breath, she shook her head. "Stop apologizing. I probably blew this out—"

"No," Noah said firmly. "You were right. I shouldn't have gone behind your back and asked Jason to check the bank incident out. It was a reflex action but you're right. You're not a job to manage or a problem on the ranch."

"Well...good, then. We understand one another."

"We do. Hey, we made it through our first fight," Noah laughed. "That was pretty good."

Liz smiled in return. "We did do well, didn't we? I'm actually impressed. We had a disagreement, we talked about it, and we came up with a plan going forward. No butt hurt feelings, no whining, just talking it out. Look at us...adulting like pros."

They were both grinning like crazy and then Liz's smile fell, her shoulders dropping.

"Shit, for a moment I forgot the whole point on this conversation. He's gone."

"He can't hurt you anymore."

She rubbed the side of her face and groaned softly. "I've let him and his friends haunt my dreams for a long time. It's hard to believe that he's dead."

"He's definitely dead. Jason confirmed it. He's not going to get out of prison and come after you. You don't have to afraid."

Placing her hands on the table, she sat up straighter in the booth. "I kept seeing his evil grin over and over in my nightmares."

Noah had read the transcripts of the trial. She hadn't told him every detail.

"He singled you out, didn't he?"

"Yes." Her gaze traveled to the window again and he waited while she gathered her thoughts. Eventually, she turned back, her lips turned down at the corners. "I don't know why."

"Probably because you're an attractive woman."

"There were other attractive women."

From what the transcripts read, McGuire had kept Liz with him the entire time in the bank vault, making her sit beside him and telling everyone that when the time came she would choose the first person to be shot. Like she was his girlfriend and accomplice. He'd tried to pull her into his savage little game.

"Maybe he liked brunettes. We'll never know except that what he did was sick and evil."

"Sick and evil," she echoed softly. "That sums it all up, doesn't it? The whole situation."

"There are bad people in the world, and they do bad things. Luckily, there are far more good."

"There are," Liz agreed. "I just can't help but wonder what turned him that way. What made him the way he was? Was he born that way or was he made?"

"That's the age-old question. Nature or nurture? I don't have the answer except to say that Jason told me that the whole family lacks a moral compass. McGuire's brother and father are both living on the wrong side of the law."

"His mother was there every day of the trial. She loved her son and she cried when they sentenced him to prison. I don't think she wanted to believe that he'd done those things."

Noah was a tad cynical about McGuire's mother sitting in court every day crying when people said mean things about him.

But I'm a cynical asshole anyway.

"Twelve people on a jury said that he did," Noah finally replied, keeping his more skeptical thoughts to himself. "A bunch of eyewitnesses said he did—hell, his own accomplices said that he did. Whether she believes it or not is on her, but I can see why she'd be upset. Her youngest son was going to prison. But I do know that none of this was your fault. None of it. And I hope this news will give you some of the closure you didn't get with the trial."

"Closure," she sighed with an eyeroll. "My therapist was big into that. This is the end of some of it, though. I've been dreading going to his parole hearings in the future. I don't have to worry about that."

"And the others? What about them?"

"I know they're just as guilty, but I barely saw them at the bank and then they pleaded guilty. For some reason…"

Her voice trailed away but Noah understood.

"They didn't make the impression on you that McGuire did?"

"That's an understatement."

"He's gone now. He can't hurt you anymore," Noah repeated. "This can be a brand-new start for you, if you want it to be."

She raised her eyes to him, a smile growing on her beautiful face. "I do want that. I want it all. I'm sick and tired of being afraid. I didn't realize how bad it was until Mallory pointed it out to me. I want to be more like the person that I was before. She lived life to the fullest."

Noah grinned and waggled his brows. "She certainly did."

"Noah Anderson, are you thinking about sex?" she asked in a mock scolding tone. "I'm shocked, absolutely shocked."

"Would you be even more shocked if I asked you back to my place after lunch?"

"Do I get dessert first?"

Fuck yes.

"We can even get it to go, if you prefer."

Chocolate cake in bed was always fun.

"Then I accept your offer. I do have to be back at the house in a couple of hours."

"That should be fine. I'm not as young as I used to be, honey."

But she sure as hell made him feel that way.

Chapter Eighteen

"WE ALWAYS SEEM to be in a hurry," Liz panted as she backed into Noah's bedroom, his arms around her, nipping her neck. They'd scrambled out of his truck and kissed all the way into the house. "We have such good intentions, too."

Blown to hell.

"We should slow down," Noah agreed in between kisses. His lips grazed her earlobe before sliding down to where neck met shoulder. She tightened her grip on his shoulders as her knees weakened. He was far too skillful. "Take our time."

But they didn't seem to be doing that. Both of them were tugging at clothes and tossing them aside like old newspapers. By the time they hit the mattress they were both naked.

She was desperate for him, wanted him badly. They had two years to make up for after all, but...

She wanted to savor this beautiful man lying on top of her, his delicious weight pressing her into the bed. There was something so incredibly sexy about his larger body almost protecting her own. It made her feel small and delicate when in reality she wasn't either of those things.

With her palms on his chest, Liz gently pushed him to his

back. For a moment, he protested but then meekly allowed her to straddle him, pillowing his head on his hands.

"What are you planning, babe?"

"We're going to slow down a little," Liz replied firmly. "I thought we could start here."

"Here?" he teased with a sizzlingly evil grin. "I can't wait to see where *here* is."

"Here can be many places."

It wasn't that Liz had never taken the lead in the bedroom…she had, but it wasn't an everyday sort of occurrence. Summoning her confidence, she leaned down and brushed their lips together, enjoying the feel of his soft mouth against hers. She thought about deepening the kiss, but there was far too much territory to be covered and she couldn't wait to explore every inch of the gorgeous male specimen spread out like a buffet in front of her.

Dropping kisses along his jawline, she traveled down his neck and across his collarbone, her tongue darting out to taste the salty skin. Her fingertips glided down his muscled arms, and she delighted in the stark differences between them – his golden skin contrasting with her much fairer complexion, his body hard and hers much softer.

He moved restlessly underneath her as she trailed kisses down his torso, stopping every now and then to give a flat male nipple a lick or to run her tongue along the ridges of his stomach. His groans and sighs gave her the confidence to keep going farther south but she paused when she reached his treasure trail, the silky path of hair that led down to his cock.

"You're not stopping now, are you?" he asked, his voice

strained.

"I am definitely not stopping."

Running her fingers over his thighs, she lightly scraped the flesh with her nails as she leaned down to give him a lick from root to tip, enjoying the way his entire body jerked in reaction and then a hiss through his gritted teeth.

"Fuck," he rasped, his hand clasping the back of her head, the fingers flexing against her scalp.

"We'll do that in a few minutes. But first I want to do this."

This was taking was him so deep in her mouth he bumped the back of her throat. Then slowly pulling back, keeping as much suction as she possibly could so there was a push-pull action that she hoped he'd like. From the way he was fisting the sheets and groaning, she was on the right track.

Over and over she sunk back down, taking all that she could, and then pulled back until only the head was in her mouth. She'd swirl her tongue a few times and then start all over again. His back was arched and his hips were lifted off the mattress, his fingers buried deeply in her hair. She was getting ready to do it again when his hand cupped her cheek.

"No more, babe. I don't want this to be over so soon."

She didn't either, to be honest. She wanted them to slow down and enjoy each other, but it wasn't easy. The entire time she'd been going down on him she was already thinking about how well he'd fill her up.

"We're going to take this slow," Liz replied, running her hands up his chest. "Take our time."

"I don't think that's going to work out."

She didn't have time to reply.

Before she could open her mouth, she was flat on her back with a happy and very aroused male hovering above her. His body brushed hers and her breath hitched as heat swept through her veins.

"I wasn't done," she protested weakly. She'd been enjoying herself but she could feel her arousal rising as images of what he might have in mind filled her brain. "I had more planned."

Leaning down, Noah pressed a kiss to the corner of her mouth and then several more down her neck. Her heart skipped a beat and then accelerated in her chest, leaving her breathless. "You'll have to save it for next time. You did too good of a job."

It was hard to concentrate when his tongue was tracing patterns on the skin between her breasts.

"Too good?"

"Too good," he repeated, nipping at the flesh and then immediately soothing it with his tongue. His fingers ghosted over her hip and then between her legs only for a moment. Just enough to make her crazy with need. "I didn't want to be selfish and make this all about me. I have things I want to do, too."

Who am I to object?

His head dipped and he nuzzled at her breast before lapping at an already hard nipple, taking it into his mouth and running his tongue around it before lightly scraping the sides with his teeth. He repeated this on the other side until she was writhing on the sheets, twisting underneath him and digging her fingers into the muscles of his back.

"Now," she whispered, hooking her leg around his waist to pull him *closer*. "Now, Noah."

The world was still spinning as Noah reached into the drawer next to the bed and rolled on protection. She'd barely noticed but then he was pushing inside of her, sinking deep and rubbing all the little sensitive spots that made her gasp and moan.

All of their couplings had been quick and frenzied, their desire too out of control to be tamed. Not this time. Noah languidly fucked her like he had all damn day to do it, slowly pulling out and then thrusting back in, their gazes locked together the entire time. His pupils were blown wide and his jaw tight, holding himself in check.

They moved together, finding the rhythm that would send them both over the edge. Each stroke drove Liz's arousal higher, heat pooling in her lower belly. When her climax hit, it was as if the world splintered apart and whirled around her in shiny pieces before coming together again. Time seemed to slow down as she watched Noah fall over the cliff as well, growling in pure male satisfaction.

Eventually they collapsed together, neither able to speak yet and both sucking oxygen into their starved lungs. Noah pulled the sheet over their rapidly cooling bodies, and Liz cuddled closer, resting her head on his chest. Under her ear she could hear the rapid beat of his heart, so strong and solid.

Was this love?

And if it was, was she *ready* to love? Could she do this?

She had a funny feeling that her answer didn't matter in the least.

Ready or not…here she was. She wouldn't blow this second chance.

Chapter Nineteen

A WEEK LATER Liz couldn't believe how different her life had become. She was happier, more relaxed, and less vigilant. She wasn't constantly checking the cameras around her house in Denver or looking over her shoulder when walking down the street. She didn't immediately assess danger when walking into a store or restaurant.

She *still* did all of those things, but much less often. It was a start.

Part of it was the news about Kenneth McGuire, but it was also the way Noah and the small community of Tremont made her feel.

There were few secrets in a town this size. People she'd never met smiled and waved at her. They asked her—by name—how the wedding preparations were coming. She might not know them but they knew her. While it took some getting used to – everyone knowing her business without her having to say a word – it also felt sort of warm and cozy. Friendly, and completely different than how she felt in Denver.

She had lovely neighbors at home but the whole darn city didn't know what she was doing and who she was doing it with.

Here in Tremont, it was clear that everyone had already paired her up with Noah. They all seemed happy about it too, which was a plus.

"Stay here awhile and you won't think this is so cool," Noah warned her over a shared piece of apple pie at the diner. They didn't have much time together today as the bachelor and bachelorette parties were tonight. They'd been trying to spend as much time together as possible but with the wedding coming up, it hadn't been easy. "What you call small town curiosity, I call nosy neighbors."

Liz had learned a great deal about this man in the last week. She'd learned that he loved a juicy steak cooked medium rare. He loved classic rock from the seventies and he thought watching baseball on television was boring. He much preferred attending a game in person. He loved to wear his blue jeans, and he had a wicked sweet tooth. He adored being outside and hated being cooped up in the house for too long. He was energetic but could veg out watching a movie in the evening. He liked to read mysteries and he loved roller coasters.

She'd found that out by accident when they'd talked about perhaps taking a short vacation together. It turned out he was a roller coaster aficionado, and had ridden most of them all across the country. It had been with a heavy heart that she'd told him she was afraid of heights and he'd drag her dead, cold, lifeless body on a coaster. She wasn't going. Period. End of subject. But she'd happily find a shady bench at whatever amusement park they were at, sit her ass down, and wait for him while he rode.

He'd simply laughed and told her that riding wasn't mandatory, although she was really missing out. As long as she didn't mind waiting, they could ride the merry-go-round when he was done.

She'd also learned that while he might complain about living in a small town in the middle of nowhere, he loved it. He'd never live anywhere else.

"Those nosy neighbors care about you," she pointed out. "Right now, I'm not at home and while my neighbors might have noticed, I can assure you they're not all that concerned. If your neighbors didn't see you for a few days, they'd be worried that you had the flu or something. They'd be sending soup."

"Did you tell your neighbors that you were going on a trip?"

"I would have if I'd seen them before I left. I didn't so…no. I did have my mail and newspaper stopped."

"I think you underestimate your neighbors. They might worry. You're a woman living alone. I'd worry about you if I lived next door."

Liz shrugged. "That's the difference between small towns and big cities. I love my neighbors. They're really wonderful people and we get along great, but they tend to keep to themselves and I do, too. It's not a bad thing, it's just different. They probably think that it's a sign of respect not to be all up in my business."

Noah grinned wickedly. "Tremont is all about being all up in your business. Everyone in town knows even the most minute details about this wedding. It's crazy."

"From what I've been able to see, when an Anderson gets married it's almost like a royal wedding. Prince Carter is taking a wife and all of Tremont is going to celebrate."

A flush stained his cheeks and he rubbed at his stubbly chin. "Shit, I hate it when people talk about us like that. We're just like everyone else's family."

Right… Liz wasn't about to argue with him about this topic.

"Is the whole town invited to the wedding? I asked Mallory that question and she just groaned and hid her head in her hands so I took that as a *yes*."

"The whole town is not invited, but a good portion of it is as they're family friends."

"I'm not sure I'd be on board with that if I was the bride. I'd rather have something much smaller and more intimate."

Realizing what she'd just said, Liz snapped her mouth shut.

Don't talk about marriage and weddings. Too soon. Far too soon. Awkward.

If Noah thought she was being pushy, he didn't act it. "I agree. I'd want something small, maybe just my family and a few friends. I think that Carter and Mallory let the pressure get to them and they finally threw up their hands and basically invited everyone my parents had ever met. I think this is the biggest Anderson wedding in our generation. Even Travis didn't have this big of a wedding and he has friends all over the world. Shane and Arden had a huge wedding a few years ago though, and I didn't think I'd see anything bigger until this one."

"What about Easton and Dizzy?"

Noah's smile widened. "They had a pretty small wedding actually, but it was easily the best one I've ever been to. Dizzy's family had some sort of shaman come in and bless the couple, which of course my twin hated, because he hates everything that he didn't write down ahead of time. For food, they had an international buffet which was some of the best cuisine I'd ever eaten in my life. And the reception had a seventies disco theme which was a hoot and a half. If you haven't seen Dizzy's mom and dad getting down to 'Staying Alive', you haven't lived."

"Video or it didn't happen."

"I can dig the video out," Noah laughed. "But I warn you, it's not for the faint of heart. At least they didn't try nude yoga at the reception. You can ask the neighbors about that. They're still talking about it."

Holy shit.

"I'm terrified but I still want to see it. It sounds like the wedding this weekend is going to be a hell of a lot more boring than that one."

"We can only hope, but you never know what can happen at a wedding. Maybe one of my relatives will get drunk and jump in the cake."

Liz had a vivid image of a man in a tuxedo doing a swan dive into a five-tiered confection.

"Did you have anyone in particular in mind for that?"

"My cousin Trey has been known to do some wild shit. He'd been double-dog dared into more stupid things than all of the rest of us combined."

"Wait…there are more of you? I thought I'd met all the Andersons. Do they have a ranch, too?"

There were more? Holy hell.

"There are more," Noah confirmed with a grin. "My dad and uncle have an Anderson cousin. They don't have a cattle ranch, though. They own a chain of hotels in the Southeast and Midwest, although they're looking into expanding throughout the United States and eventually overseas. They flew in this morning so you'll get to meet them. Not tonight but definitely at the rehearsal dinner."

More Anderson men... It was an intimidating thought.

"So are you looking forward to the bachelor party tonight? Are there going to be strippers there?"

"I don't know. Are there going to be strippers at the bachelorette party?"

"I can safely say the answer is no. It's just a bunch of women going out to dinner, having a few drinks, and then some dancing. No hijinks of any kind. Mallory was adamant about this and frankly, we agree with her. We're all a little old to be getting drunk and doing things we wouldn't want on YouTube."

"I doubt Carter is going to have strippers, either. He made a remark not long ago that his entire twenties were one big bachelor party so I think he's also going to try and keep it low key. I'm guessing pizza, beer, and poker."

"Aren't you the best man?"

"Yes, but Shane wanted to take lead on the party, and I was happy to let him." Noah leaned forward, his eyes twinkling. "And baby, I am the best man."

"You certainly don't lack self-esteem, Noah Anderson."

"It's one of my better qualities," he boasted, his chest puffed out with pride. "I think you like it."

She was sure he was right. She was beginning to like every single thing about this man.

It should have scared her, but it didn't.

It felt...perfect.

✦　✦　✦

"IF I HAVE a stripper Mallory will kill me," Carter declared with a laugh. "She'll enjoy every damn minute of it, too. That was our one agreement. No strippers for either of us."

Shane had surprised them all and rented out the local watering hole for the bachelor party. There was food from the barbecue joint down the road and all the alcoholic beverages they could drink. Most of the men had broken off into groups to play poker while a basketball game played silently on the televisions around the room.

Their cousin Ace – his real name was Alden but he hated it – tossed down three cards. They were playing five card stud. "It wouldn't bother me if my woman had a stripper. I'm secure. Don't you trust Mallory?"

Noah was dealing and he dealt three cards to Ace. "I don't think it's a matter of trust so much as I wouldn't want some guy's junk all up in Liz's face, either. I trust that she wouldn't do anything but I can't say the same for him."

"I trust Mallory," Carter replied. "Totally. But like Noah said, I don't know if I trust the stripper in the scenario. Plus, he's right. I don't want some guy all up in Mallory's business."

Shane tossed down his cards. "I'm out. This hand is too rich for my blood, but for the rest of you, I think Noah is bluffing."

Noah flipped his brother the bird. "Fuck you, brother. You don't know when I'm bluffing. You only wish you did. You are without a doubt the worst poker player in the history of the Anderson family. Bar none. You're terrible."

Shane didn't look too bothered by his older brother's accusation. If anything, he appeared amused, his smile almost mocking.

"That's because I have better fucking things to do than to

hang out in honky-tonks drinking whiskey and playing cards."

At one point in Shane's life he had been considered the wild one in the family, so that statement from him had everyone at the table rolling with laughter.

"I know why he's a terrible player," their cousin Trey said with a smirk. He was younger brother to Ace, and they were brothers to Grant and Justin who were at another table playing poker with West, Travis, and Zach. Easton wasn't allowed to play poker with the family anymore because he was really good at it. As in really, really good. He couldn't help it. It was simply how his brain worked. "Because he can't concentrate on the game. His mind is wondering what Arden is doing."

"I think we're all wondering what our women are doing," Carter admitted. "Leanne said that she was taking them out for a nice meal and then they were going to go dancing."

"But she didn't say where she was taking them," Noah added. "Where are they going to go dancing around here?"

That had sort of been bugging him all evening. He couldn't imagine where they had gone. There weren't that many places in Tremont to party, and Shane had already rented out the main one. Where were the ladies?

"Do you think they went to Billings?" Ace asked. "There's places to go dancing there."

"Maybe Leanne rented one of those party buses," Trey offered. "That's what we should have done."

Shane poured them all another shot of whiskey. "What's wrong with this place? Are you saying that you're not having any fun?"

"I'm having fun," Trey protested, throwing back the shot.

"Jesus, you're uptight since getting married. You used to be a hell of a lot more relaxed. In Florida we're not this tightly wound."

"I am not–"

Ace held up his hands and shook his head. "Do not engage with him, Shane. He can do this all fucking night. He'll make you crazy if you let him. Trey likes to fuck with people just for laughs. If he gets on your nerves, just do what I do. Punch him. He can take it."

Noah's cousins were known to be rowdy and loud, especially with one another. His mom had always said that they were just born a little a wilder than most, but that their hearts were twice as big.

"I am not wound tightly," Shane muttered, pouring Trey another shot of whiskey. "Have a fucking drink, asshole."

Out of the corner of his eye, Noah saw Jason at the bar filling his plate with food from the buffet. He wanted to thank his cousin again for getting the information about Kenneth McGuire. While Liz had been angry at first, she'd been visibly more relaxed in the last few days since hearing that the man responsible for her trauma was dead.

"Excuse me, gentlemen. I need to stretch my legs for a few minutes."

Noah pushed back his chair and headed for Jason, who was now sitting on a bar stool and enjoying a pulled pork sandwich.

"Hey, I just wanted to say thank you again for digging into the bank robbery. I do think she feels better knowing he can't get out and hurt her."

Wiping his hands on a paper napkin, Jason took a drink of

his beer. "It wasn't any trouble. I'm glad that it helped. Liz seems like a nice woman, and what happened to her was particularly nasty. She's obviously a strong person to go through that and come out the other side."

Noah couldn't help but think that Jason was pretty damn strong, too. After all, he'd survived being a prisoner of a deadly drug cartel. He didn't talk about it but he was definitely a changed man, and in many of the same ways that Liz had changed.

They were both quieter, more watchful, more alert. They were cautious, not jumping into anything right away until they had the lay of the land. Like Liz, Jason assessed every building or situation he walked into for danger. Perhaps they always would. They'd been through something that Noah would never completely understand.

"She is a strong woman, and she's come a long way since she was taken hostage. I just want to do all I can to help her."

"Just let me know if you need my help again. I'm happy to do it." Jason nodded toward the table Noah had just vacated. "How's your luck tonight?"

"Ace is taking all of our money and I swear Trey is in on it, trying to distract us. Does he ever shut up?" Noah chuckled.

Jason barked with laughter. "He does, but it wouldn't surprise me if they were working together. The one you have to watch out for is Justin. He never says a goddamn word but all of the sudden your pockets are empty, your girlfriend is sitting on his lap, and you're left wondering what in the fuck just happened."

"I take it this is from personal experience?"

"It was spring break my junior year in college," Jason explained with a grin. Whatever memories he had certainly weren't painful. "Like all us Montana Andersons, we traveled down to Florida for some sun and warm weather whenever we could and my girlfriend at the time came with me that year. Like always, we stayed with our aunt and uncle and the first few days it was great. We were having fun and everything was fine. Then Grant decides he wants to throw a party and there must have been about a hundred college kids in that backyard. We were shoulder to shoulder. I went inside to grab some food in the kitchen and when I came out my girlfriend was slow dancing with Justin. At first, I didn't think much about it but as the night went on it was clear that she preferred him to me."

Noah had never heard this story but it was clear that Jason didn't harbor a broken heart. He was having a hard time telling the story because he was laughing so hard.

"So what did you do?"

"What could I do? I yelled at Justin and took a swing at him, of course. Then he took a swing at me, too. His dad came out and separated us while his mom put ice on our matching black eyes. Then his dad took us into his den and laid some major wisdom down on us. He said that any girl that would jump from one guy to another in one single evening probably wasn't anyone that either one of us should be thinking about long-term. Damn, he had a point. So I broke up with her the next morning and Justin didn't pay her any more attention. She sulked for the next few days, and during the entire flight back home she kept trying to tell me that she was sorry but that Justin was just so charming and funny. He made her feel special, she said. Since then I've never underestimated the power of your cousin Justin with women. He doesn't even try. It's really something to see."

Noah snuck a glance at the cousin in question who was quietly playing poker at a table in the corner. He didn't look like some major Casanova. Sure, he was good-looking but he wasn't a movie star or anything. He was a numbers dude, just like Noah's twin Easton. Justin was a good guy and everyone loved him, but Noah didn't see a babe magnet when he looked at his cousin.

But I'm not a female.

"Justin? I guess I don't see it."

"It's the quiet ones you have to watch out for. They sneak under the radar."

"You're not holding a grudge, right?"

Jason's face split into a grin. "Are you kidding? He saved my ass. When I look back, that girl was nothing but misery. I should be thanking him."

"How did we even start talking about this?"

"You were complaining about losing your ass to Ace."

Right.

"I don't think I'm going to be lucky in cards tonight."

"Better to be lucky in love. If you ask me, that is."

Jason was a wise man. Poker was fine, but Liz? She was better than anyone he'd ever known.

Chapter Twenty

SINCE LEANN WAS local, Liz, Celia, and Dani had been happy to hand over the reins of the bachelorette party. There had only been one caveat from Mallory...

No strippers. She and Carter had made an agreement.

Which was fine by the other women in the group, especially Liz. She'd attended a few bachelorette parties in the past and she hadn't found the male strippers all that attractive, nor did she want one gyrating in her face. She wasn't a prude by any stretch but it simply wasn't her thing. If other women wanted to shake their booty with a guy in a g-string? Go for it and more power to them.

Life was short and a person should do whatever they wanted as long as they didn't hurt anyone else. If her friends wanted to stick dollar bills in a guy's junk, she'd be sitting right beside them, cheering them on. Hell, she might even pass them a handful of Washingtons, but the dancer needed to keep a decent distance from her.

Now if Noah wanted to give her a little dance as he tugged off his clothes... that would a completely different situation. She'd stomp, catcall, and generally be all in favor of that. She might even toss away a few articles of her own clothing.

Did that make her a hypocrite? Probably.

The group hadn't a clue what Leann had in mind for tonight. The original plan had been a movie night but Leann had said they needed to do something bigger and more special. She'd mentioned good food, music, and dancing which they were all excited for. What she hadn't told them was that she was going to use the atrium at Anderson Industries for the festivities. The building was deserted, save for a few security guards, there was plenty of parking, and lots of space. Because the office was in a downtown area there were also no nearby residents to hear them if the party got rowdy later on.

The dinner had been catered by the best steakhouse in Montana and they'd all sat down to a perfectly prepared meal and amazing service by white-gloved waiters. The tablescapes were beautiful with white linen tablecloths, gleaming china and crystal, and pink baby roses for the centerpieces. Lit candles were on every surface, reflecting off the glass walls that overlooked the leafy green courtyard. This was a bachelorette party with class. right down to the chocolate mousse for dessert.

"Leann, you did a wonderful job putting this together," Liz said, taking her last bite of mousse. She should have stopped eight or nine bites ago but it was simply too good to not eat the whole thing. She was going to have to be rolled out the front doors later. "Everything is so delicious. I shouldn't have eaten so much."

"You can burn it off later when the tables are put away and the music comes on." Leann pointed up to the ceiling. "Did you see that I bought a giant disco ball? I wanted this party to be over the top."

"You've succeeded."

"I just wanted to welcome Mallory to our crazy family and thank her for making me part of the wedding without actually having to be a bridesmaid." Leann's hand flew to her mouth. "Wait, that didn't come out right. I would have been happy to be a bridesmaid, but it's just that I think that at a certain point a female should retire from it after being in a certain amount of weddings."

Liz had a vision of that movie...what was it called? Something about a bunch of dresses?

"How many weddings have you been in?"

"I lost count after twenty. At that point, I donated the dresses to charity and never looked back."

"I don't have near that many friends. That's a lot of dresses and matching shoes."

Leann rolled her eyes. "And all the pink. I actually like pink but I wore a lot of it. And pastels. So many pastels. My second closet looked like a unicorn exploded in there."

"Were you in Dizzy's wedding?"

"I was, but believe me when I say that the dress I wore wasn't traditional in any sense. Nor was the wedding."

"Mallory let us pick our own dresses as long as we stayed in the color scheme."

"And that's just one of the ways that Mallory is fantastic. How did you meet?"

Smiling at the memory, Liz recounted that first day of college.

"All four of us were assigned to the same dorm suite. It was one of those with two bedrooms with two people in each bedroom, a living room area and a bathroom. We were all freshman and very nervous. Well, three of us were nervous. Dani wasn't nervous because she's never nervous. But anyway, we were assigned to live together and I guess we didn't have to become best friends, but we did. From almost the first moment I felt super comfortable with them and we just started doing everything together. Now I can't imagine my life without them. They're the kind of friends who will drop their own lives to be there for you when you need them, and I hope that they feel the same about me because I've tried to do the same. We've all said that when we get old, we want to be four gray-haired women rocking on the front porch of some big old house."

Leann nodded knowingly. "That's the kind of friendship that I have with Dizzy. She can practically read my mind. We even finish each other's sentences."

"It's great to have that kind of connection with–"

Liz's attention was captured by one of the waiters clearing a nearby table. Her heart stuttered in her chest and it was suddenly difficult to take a breath. He looked like...

Kenneth McGuire.

"Are you okay?" Leann asked, her tone filled with concern. Her gaze followed Liz's. "Is everything alright? Do you know him?"

The man, dressed in a catering uniform and his arms filled with dirty dessert dishes, disappeared into the Anderson Industries cafeteria kitchen. Staring at the closed door, Liz shook her head and blinked a few times trying to clear her vision.

What the actual fuck?

"No, I don't know him. He just…looked like someone I used to know."

Leann frowned. "Are you sure it's not him? The lighting in here isn't great."

McGuire was dead so it couldn't be him. This was her brain playing tricks on her. For a few months after the robbery, she'd thought she saw him all over Denver but of course it never was him. He'd been in jail and now he was gone.

She hadn't had these visions though for over a year and a half. Why now?

"It can't be him. He's…passed on. It just looked a lot like him, that's all. I was just surprised for a moment."

"They say everyone has a twin. Maybe you found his."

That was possible. It was also possible that her imagination was having a field day with her.

But why now? Just when she was making progress? Was she the kind of person that had to create drama where there wasn't any? And if she was, what did that say about her? Nothing good, that was for sure.

Kenneth McGuire was dead. He couldn't hurt her anymore.

She needed to get herself under control because frankly, if she kept doing this…she was only hurting herself.

LIZ WAS DOING it again.

Looking over her shoulder. Assessing the room for possible dangers. Eyeing any strangers, studying the faces and the way people moved. Looking for…something. At this point, she wasn't even sure what the hell she thought she would find, but she was back there in the abyss once more and hating every single second of it. What had happened to her tonight? She'd been so happy only a few hours ago.

She'd even pulled her handbag closer, so that her weapon of choice would only be inches away if she needed it.

Why would I even need it? I'm at a party with friends and there's security guards at the door.

There was a security guard at the bank, too.

"Come dancing," Mallory called from the dance floor, waving her arms in the air. Celia and Dani were dancing as well. That disco ball was spinning, sending shots of light all over the large room. "Come on. You know you love this song."

Liz did love this song but…

What do I say? That I'm scared again? Shit.

Dani leaned over to say something in Mallory's ear and then came to sit next to Liz at the table. "What's going on? Your trick knee acting up?"

"I don't have a trick knee."

Dani knew it, too.

"Then I can't imagine why you wouldn't want to join us on the dance floor where we are acting like complete fools. I promise you it will be fun."

Liz couldn't help it. Her gaze darted to her purse on the table before returning to her friend. Dani, of course, immediately picked up on it.

"You don't want to leave your purse? Is that it?"

Her tone was neutral, not judging in any way, but Liz felt the burn of shame. Tears burned the backs of her eyes and her fingers tightened on the leather strap.

"Why don't you tell me what's wrong and then we can try and work on this."

This was the worst. She hated herself right now because she was tired of being scared all the damn time. She wanted to have fun and be free.

What's wrong with me?

"I thought I saw him."

Liz's voice sounded rusty, as if she hadn't used her vocal cords in a long time.

Dani patted her hand, leaning closer so that Liz wouldn't have to speak up.

"Saw who, hon?"

"Him. Kenneth McGuire." The words had to be pushed by force out of her mouth. "I thought one of the waiters was him but of course it can't be. He's dead. It's my fucking mind playing tricks on me and not letting me be happy. Why can't I let myself be happy?"

A few tears did fall and Liz brushed them away quickly, not wanting anyone else to know that she was crying. Again. Tears hadn't helped much in the past and they wouldn't tonight, either.

Dani squeezed Liz's hand, her expression one of sympathy and love. "Sweetie, it's going to take some time before your brain believes that he's really gone. You only learned this a few days ago. You've been scared for so long that I think feeling this way might even be a habit for you. That isn't going to be easy to break."

Liz wanted to throw up her hands in despair. "I was fine just a few hours ago and now I'm a mess again. I hate this. I just want to be normal."

Dani's eyes widened comically and she shook her head frantically. "Don't ever let me hear that you want to be normal ever again. I can't think of anything more horrid than to be normal. How incredibly boring. Our quirks and flaws are what make us interesting."

"Then I must be one of the most interesting people that you know," Liz replied dryly. "I'm fucking fascinating."

"You are," Dani agreed. "Stop being so hard on yourself. You've made so much progress and you're mad because you're not perfect yet. You need to give yourself a break. We're proud of you and how hard you've worked to overcome what happened, but I think that it's sad that you can't be proud of yourself. You should be."

"How can you be proud of me when I can't leave my purse?"

"Because a year ago you wouldn't have realized that it was even an issue."

Such a simple statement but there was a load of truth in it.

"I might have realized it but I wouldn't have admitted it."

"See? Progress. Now how about coming out onto the dance floor with us? Tomorrow you'll be sad that you sat here all night while everyone else had a good time." Dani let go of her hand and pointed to the purse. "Sling that bad boy over your shoulder and come join us."

"I can't do that," Liz protested, her cheeks burning with new embarrassment. It was bad enough that her close friends knew she had problems. She didn't need Mallory's new family and friends to know too. "Everyone will–"

"What?" Dani cut in. "They'll do what? They aren't going to

do shit because most of us are too drunk, to be honest. Anyone else can go pound sand as far as I am concerned. If you want to bring that purse out onto the dance floor then you should do it. No judgments. Screw anyone else."

With all the strength that Liz could muster, she slowly and deliberately unfurled her fingers where they were gripping the soft leather strap, letting it dangle off the edge of the round table.

"I can leave it here. It's okay."

"Hon, you don't have to do that."

Dani understood a lot but she couldn't possibly understand this. Liz barely understood it.

"I do have to do it."

Dani nodded to a small table by the dance floor where a few candles burned. "Why don't you put it there? It will be right there for you if you need it."

Relief flooded Liz's body, and she almost sagged against the chair as she blew out a breath.

"That...that would be good."

"Then let's do that." Dani stood and held out her hand. "Ready to get down?"

Maybe, but Liz wasn't going to allow her fear to win. Not tonight. Not when she was with her friends. This one time she was going to be stronger.

Three steps forward, two steps back. It was still progress.

But did it have to be so damn slow?

Chapter Twenty-One

Later that evening, Noah pulled open the glass doors of Anderson Industries and strode into the dimly lit lobby. The men at the bachelor party had found out the women were in the atrium dancing up a storm via a text from Dizzy to Easton. They'd immediately wrangled the designated drivers – Easton, Grant, and West – and headed straight over.

By the time they arrived, the whiskey and beer Noah had consumed earlier had worn off but it had left him a slightly sleepy. Holding Liz close on the dance floor while a slow ballad played sounded like the perfect way to end an evening out.

There was a disco ball. *A disco ball.* Loud music and lots of women on the dance floor. There were streamers and horns, as if it was New Year's Eve, and Mallory wore a sparkly tiara that continually caught the rotating lights. There was also a midnight dessert buffet and a huge bucket full of ice and champagne bottles.

When Mallory saw Carter, she raised her arms and grinned with glee. "It's my future lawfully wedded husband."

Carter lifted her up and spun her around. "I couldn't stay away from you, baby."

His bride giggled and pressed a kiss to his lips. "Naturally. Come dance with me."

The ladies didn't seem a bit perturbed that their party had been crashed by a bunch of guys. If anything, they were welcomed with open arms and a rousing cheer. A few of the men took straight to the dance floor including Carter and Trey, showing off whatever moves they had while Easton and Ace went straight for the food.

Liz emerged from the crowded dance floor and linked her arm with his. "I didn't expect to see you here tonight. Did you and the guys get lonely?"

"We did. It's pathetic, I know, but frankly we got tired of playing poker and smoking cigars."

Her cute little nose wrinkled and she gave his shirt a sniff. "I hate the smell of cigars."

"I didn't smoke any but a few of the others did. To be honest, I'm not fond of them, either." He glanced around at the party still in full swing. "Are you having a good time, honey? It looks like Leann pulled out all the stops for this one."

He'd meant it as an idle question but it was easy to see that Liz wasn't comfortable with it. She avoided meeting his gaze, looking everywhere but at him. "She did a great job. The meal was catered and it was excellent. Are you hungry? There's a dessert buffet. Or I could get you some champagne. Or there's other drinks, too. Are you thirsty?"

He wouldn't have minded a glass of water but now all he wanted was to find out why Liz was acting so strangely. Those few sentences had been spoken so fast it was like they were shot out of cannon.

"Is everything okay? You seem a little out of sorts, honey."

Liz sort of curled in on herself, her handbag pressed against her body. It was then that he realized what was going on. Had she been carrying it around all night?

"Why don't we go somewhere quieter and you can tell me about it, okay?"

She nodded, and he led her down the hall and into a large conference room. The music from the atrium could still be heard along with voices and laughter but they'd at least be able to hear themselves think.

He pulled out a brown leather chair and urged her to sit down, while he did the same, scooting close so their knees were touching. Leaning forward, he captured her hands and tangled their fingers together.

"I see that you've got your purse."

He kept any judgment out of his tone, not wanting her to think that he thought badly of her for doing it. He was simply surprised. Since the news of McGuire's death, she'd seemed so much more carefree and far less nervous and suspicious.

Liz cast a glance down at the purse which was tucked next to her on the chair. "I can explain."

"You don't have to explain anything to me if you don't want to. I'm just concerned, that's all."

Sighing, she let her head fall back against the high-back cushion. "I thought I saw him tonight. It sort of sent me into a tailspin."

"You thought you saw him? Here?"

She nodded. "I thought I saw him clearing the tables after dinner. Before you tell me that Kenneth McGuire is dead and that he's probably not moonlighting as a busboy in Tremont, Montana in the afterlife, I know that he's dead. But apparently my brain hasn't quite got the message yet. Dani thinks it's because that I've taken such a giant step forward and my subconscious is sort of freaking out. Being scared is my safe place. Doesn't that sound pathetic?"

Noah made a mental note to thank Dani when he had the chance because what she said made absolute perfect sense. It made so much sense, in fact, that he should have predicted that something like this would happen. Liz had been living in a self-imposed prison for a long time and her mind wasn't going to give that up easily. It would put up a fight.

"I do not think that you sound pathetic at all, and I think your friend Dani is a genius. We all should have seen this coming and prepared for it. This isn't going to magically go away just because McGuire is dead."

"I was sort of counting on that, though."

"So was I but we're back to reality." He reached out and tentatively placed a hand on her purse. "So that's why you wanted this with you?"

"It made me feel safer." She lifted her stubborn chin. "I won't ever be a victim again."

With all his heart and soul, Noah hoped that was the case. He couldn't imagine his life without this woman in it. He'd crossed over a line in their relationship and he wasn't looking back.

"Why am I so fixated on him? There were other criminals there that day."

"Because he was fixated on you," Noah replied. "Because you

had to go through his trial while the others pled guilty. It's only natural that he would be the one that would haunt you more."

She sighed, her lips turned down in sadness. "I'm so tired of this. I don't want to live my life like this anymore."

"That's good. It's that desire that's going to keep you moving forward." He levered far enough out of his chair to lean over and brush her lips with his own. "I'll be there with you. You won't be alone."

Sniffling, she rubbed the back of her hand against her eyes. "Stop it. You're going to make me cry. And I'm tired of doing that, too."

"Then how about we go dance? I'm not that coordinated but I can manage a few steps."

She ran her fingertips over his stubbled jaw and he nuzzled into her hand, loving the feeling of her satin skin against his far rougher flesh. "You're a good dancer."

"I'm an okay dancer. Now what do you say?" He tapped the handbag. "It can come, too. It's fine."

He could see that it wasn't fine. Not to her. She was biting her lip and her normally light brown eyes were almost grey with conflict.

"I can set it on the table," she finally said. "I did that before. I feel very safe when you're here."

Did she have any idea what that simple statement did to him? His chest tightened painfully and there didn't feel like there was enough room for his heart anymore. He might as well give it to her. Piece by piece, she was slowly owning it. This was fate and the universe, after all. Who was he to fight it?

"Thank you."

He managed to get the words out despite barely being able to breathe. If this was going to become a habit, he was in trouble.

"I need to freshen up."

Noah stood, lending her a helping hand as well. "There's a ladies room on the way back."

They walked hand in hand back to the party, stopping at the restroom on the way. Like most large get-togethers, the bathrooms were busy with people coming and going.

"Go on. I'll meet you when I'm done."

He didn't want to leave her, not when she was feeling so vulnerable.

"I'll just wait here–"

"No, I'll be fine. It's okay," she pressed, giving him her best brave smile. "There's lots of people around. Go get us a couple of sodas and I'll be right there. Five minutes tops."

As much as he didn't want to leave her, he also didn't want to make her think that she couldn't handle herself. Or worse, that *he* didn't think she could take care of herself.

"Take your time," he said, finally capitulating. "I'll get us a couple of ginger ales and meet you on the dance floor."

"Sounds good."

Liz disappeared into the ladies room and Noah headed into the crowded atrium. He easily located the drinks and grabbed two cans of soda from a large ice filled chest.

"Paper cups?"

A smiling older woman wearing a catering uniform was holding out two paper cups.

"Thanks. That would be great."

Her gaze ran over the dancers under the disco ball. "Seems

like a fun party. There's going to be a wedding, right?"

"There is. This weekend."

True to her word, Liz was already walking toward him. So incredibly gorgeous. He couldn't drag his eyes from her.

"She's very beautiful," the woman observed. "You're a lucky man."

"I am, thank you."

He was. Luck might have brought them together the first and second time, but he wasn't going to depend on it going forward. Noah was going to do everything he possibly could to make sure that this time they stayed together.

Chapter Twenty-Two

THERE WERE A bunch of hungover people at breakfast the next morning. Most of the group met at the diner, although a few had stayed back to get some extra sleep.

Liz had thought about staying in bed and pulling the covers over her head but her friends were determined that she wasn't going to get away with that. According to them, if Mallory could get out of bed and go to breakfast after all the booze she'd consumed, Liz could get out of bed as well.

So she'd dragged her carcass out of bed and into the shower, trying to wake up when she'd spent most of the night tossing and turning. She couldn't even blame alcohol or staying up late.

It was Kenneth McGuire's fault.

Or to put it another way…her stupid brain's fault.

He'd taken up a space in her head and he wasn't going to let it go easily. After she and her friends had come home last night, they'd all crawled into bed, groggy from good food, drink, and friends. After the long day she'd had, Liz should have fallen asleep quickly but instead she'd stayed awake running through those moments when she'd thought she'd seen him.

Over and over, beginning to question her very sanity.

It really looked like him.

But it couldn't be him. Even if he wasn't dead, he would have been in prison for a very long time.

"You look like you hate your waffle."

What?

Liz looked up from her plate and into Noah's eyes, the corners crinkled in amusement. "I don't understand."

"I said you look like you hate your waffle. Feeling hungover, babe?"

It was an excellent excuse. Too much booze. So she grabbed at it.

"A little, yes. But I don't hate the waffle. I like waffles." Her eyes narrowed as she took in Noah's handsome face. He looked like he'd slept eight hours and ate kale at every meal. What in the hell? "Why are you so bright-eyed and bushy-tailed? You drank last night, too."

Chuckling, he popped a piece of bacon into his mouth. "The famous Anderson hangover cure. It works every time."

One glance around the table told the tale. All the Anderson men looked amazing while those without their last name looked like they'd rather be back in bed. Even Mallory didn't look that great, so clearly Carter hadn't shared this secret with her. Dizzy, Leann, and the other wives, however, looked chipper and rested.

"You aren't going to share it? That's cruel."

He shrugged and sighed regretfully, although he didn't look sorry at all. "You have to be an Anderson to be let in on the secret. I'm sorry."

Asshole.

"You won't even give me a hint? And what about Mallory?

She's getting married in a few days. You won't even tell her?"

"I can't. Carter will tell her after they're married."

This had to be some sort of joke. He couldn't actually be serious.

"This is bullshit." She poked him in the chest with her finger. "I think you're full of it. Absolutely full of it. Anderson family secret? No way. More like Noah Anderson trying to pull my leg. I bet if I looked up hangover cures on the internet I'd get a better answer than from you."

"Go ahead. You won't find it. It's controversial."

"Controversial?" she echoed. More bullshit. "What do you do? Sacrifice a virgin or something? Just tell me what it is. If this is even real, which I don't think that it is."

"Then you won't care that I can't tell you."

Liz hadn't had much sleep, her eyes felt gritty, and her stomach wasn't quite up to snuff, either. It all added up to less than perfect patience. If he wouldn't answer a straight question, then she'd ask someone else.

"Leann, your cousin here says that the Anderson family has a secret hangover remedy but he won't tell me what it is. I think he's full of shit. What's the verdict?"

Dizzy's hand flew to her mouth and Brinley's face turned pink, her shoulder shaking with laughter while Jason ducked his head down, clearly trying to hide a grin. Every Anderson man around the table looked like they wanted to bust out laughing.

"The Anderson family hangover cure secret?" Leann said with a smile. "He told you about that?"

"He said it was *controversial* and that I needed to be an Anderson to know about it. I don't mind not knowing about it, but right now I'm thinking that he's playing a joke on me."

Arden was Shane's wife, beautiful but extremely quiet, barely speaking even last night at the party. She glanced around the table and then back at Liz.

"There is a secret hangover remedy," Arden said with a smirk. "It is controversial as well. Only the men do it. The women just pace ourselves when we drink, make sure to eat and stay hydrated. The usual stuff. No secrets there."

Shane shook his head, his cheeks red. "Aw, baby. Don't rat us out."

"Rat you out? This is no secret cure," Arden replied with an eyeroll. "Liz, the famous Anderson hangover cure is actually quite simple. The men drink too much, often puke, and then pretend that they're fine because they'd rather die than admit they feel like hell. I guarantee you, right now, if these men were alone they'd be whining and bellyaching about how awful they feel. So the secret is really no secret. They just pretend. In fact, in a few minutes one of these big strong strapping males is going to pretend to take a phone call when he's really going into the men's room to be sick. Later they'll all pretend to need to sit in their dens or bedrooms with the doors closed. They'll tell you they're doing paperwork when they're actually napping."

Leann elbowed her husband Zach. "Except for him. He really does have the constitution of a rhino. I've never seen anything like it. He can drink and it never affects him."

Zach grinned and nodded. "Gigi and Aubrey are the same. It's a family trait. Comes in handy every now and then."

Liz turned her attention back to her new boyfriend. "What do you have to say for yourself?"

Grimacing, he held up his phone. "That I need to take a phone call in the men's room?"

Everyone laughed, including Liz, who wrapped her arms around Noah's neck and gave him a quick peck on the cheek. "I didn't realize you were such a jokester–"

The words died in her throat as she blinked once, twice, three times. It was happening again. Her stomach curled into a knot and bile rose in her throat. She didn't want this. Not now when she was having fun and living life.

"Honey, what's wrong?"

She pointed out the large picture window of the diner. "Across the street. I saw him again, walking down the sidewalk."

To her surprise Noah shoved back his chair, the legs scraping loudly on the tile. "Then let's go find him. So you can see that it isn't him for real. Maybe that will help with this."

Dani nodded in agreement. "That's a great idea. Go quick and find him. You need to see that it's just someone who vaguely resembles him."

Liz didn't stop to ponder the suggestion, letting Noah lead her outside the diner. They jogged across the street and down to the corner as quickly as possible, but by the time they arrived there wasn't anyone there.

"He's gone."

Taking a deep breath, Liz swallowed her disappointment. She'd wanted to find him, make herself see that he wasn't McGuire.

"If there's someone walking around Tremont and looks like Kenneth McGuire, we'll find him," Noah said, his gaze running up and down the intersection. "This town just isn't that big that he can hide for long."

"Or maybe he doesn't look like McGuire. This could just be me doing this. Me being crazy."

With no end in sight.

✦   ✦   ✦

THE NEXT MORNING, Noah cornered Jason right before they were supposed to tee off on the local golf course. The ladies were having a spa day and the men were doing eighteen holes.

"Is there any possible way that Kenneth McGuire could be alive?"

Jason frowned. "What? No. No, he's dead. Why do you ask? Is this about Liz seeing someone that looked like him?"

Yes and no. Noah had been thinking about this since yesterday. Liz hadn't had this issue for months, by her own admission. And well…stranger shit had happened.

"There's no way that Kenneth McGuire could have faked his own death? It's impossible?"

Pinching the bridge of his nose, Jason sighed. "I just wanted to relax and play golf today."

"We all did, now answer the question."

Sinking down onto the locker room bench, Jason reached down to tie his shoes. "Do you know what all would be involved in faking a death inside of a state prison?"

"No, and that's why I'm asking you. Could he have done it?"

"My answer is going to be the same. No. He couldn't have done it. He'd have to have the cooperation of the prison doctor, the warden, and who knows who else. This isn't a television show—this is real life."

"People do fake their deaths," Noah persisted. "I've heard that it's happened."

Jason nodded in agreement. "It has happened, but under less stringent circumstances. McGuire was in a state prison. That means that the state of Colorado was responsible for him twenty-four-seven. Now, you could argue whether they did a good job since he was in a prison fight, but the prison doctor has to sign off on that death certificate."

"He could have been paid off."

Noah could see that he was making his cousin crazy. He wasn't doing it on purpose, but if Liz hadn't been seeing McGuire all around her for months until she came to Tremont...

"With what? How would they pay him off? McGuire didn't have any money. He was cremated by the state since his family couldn't pay for it. And while we're talking about this, let's talk about all the people that witnessed him dying. The other inmates, the guards, the prison nurse. That's a lot of people to pay off. I suppose it could be done, but it would be damn hard to do and even harder to keep under wraps. As soon as more than one or two people know what's going on, secrets have a way of becoming public knowledge."

Noah sat heavily down onto the bench, rubbing the back of his neck where he now had a pain that didn't seem to want to go away. "Liz said that right after the bank robbery she thought she saw McGuire everywhere."

"That would make sense after what she went through."

"But she hasn't for months. Then suddenly she comes here and she sees him again. Dani said it was because her subconscious is freaking out about her not wanting to be afraid all of the time. Being scared is her safe space and all of that. But I've been thinking…"

"That McGuire is alive and fucking with her," Jason finished. "That's some wild ass conjecture. The chances are slim to none. I know you want Liz to be happy and healthy but if she says she's seeing someone that looks like Kenneth McGuire, maybe she is. Not him, but someone that has his coloring or maybe walks like him. Everyone has a lookalike, right?"

"And Kenneth McGuire's lookalike just happens to live in Tremont? Those odds seem even more farfetched than faking his own death."

"I'll agree with that." Jason scraped his fingers through his short hair. "Okay, I'll call the warden. He's a friend of a friend. He's going to think I've lost my fucking mind."

The last part was muttered under Jason's breath but Noah didn't care. He was grateful that his cousin was taking this seriously.

"I'll owe you big for this."

"Yes, you will." He pulled out his phone. "Now give me a few minutes to call my friend. You know, all I wanted to do today was play golf. I'm always so busy with work I never get to play golf anymore."

"I'm thankful."

"Fuck you."

Noah stood and headed toward the locker room door. "I'll wait with the guys. If I haven't said thank you yet…thank you. I really am grateful, Jason."

"Go away."

Noah happily left his cousin alone. It was an insane theory but he had to be sure...

Was Kenneth McGuire really dead?

Chapter Twenty-Three

T HERE WAS A huge barbecue at the Anderson ranch that evening filled with family, friends, and delicious food. Liz was sure she'd never seen this much food in her entire life. There were slabs of steak, hamburgers, hot dogs, chicken, and even veggie burgers. There was an entire table of side items, in addition to a table of desserts. At the rate she was going for this wedding, she wasn't going to fit into her bridesmaid dress on the wedding day.

If only putting on a few pounds were her biggest problem.

She was ecstatic that she and Noah had reconnected, but that happiness was dimmed by the fact that she had baggage. Issues. Problems. Stuff. Things that weren't going to be solved overnight. It was bad enough that she had to deal with this, but to put Noah through it, too? He hadn't signed on for this. Sure, he kept saying that he wanted to help her but he didn't know what he was getting himself in for. She did. She'd been living this for the last two years and while it was getting better, it was still…bad. She feared she might be dealing with this for the rest of her life.

All day long she'd been looking all around her, studying the faces of strangers to see if they resembled Kenneth McGuire. To her relief and frustration, none had. But she was still doing it even now, searching for a person that she really didn't even want to see.

I don't want that. I want to move on.

Sadly, it wasn't as simple as snapping her fingers and making it all go away. But for tonight, she would paste on a smile and pretend that everything was just fine. It was the least she could do for Mallory. Liz didn't want to be the proverbial turd in the punchbowl. And she sure as hell didn't want to make this night, or any other, all about her. It was bad enough after what had happened at the bachelorette party last night.

Celia sidled up next to her, two drinks in her hand. "I got you a soda. I don't think any of us want any more alcohol tonight. In fact, I'm on the wagon until the wedding."

"Me too," Liz agreed, accepting the beverage. "I don't think I'll drink at the wedding, either. Sober is the way to go."

Celia gave her a knowing look. "You're not carrying it today. That's good."

The purse, of course.

"I left it in the house."

"Progress, but you need to cut yourself some slack. If I'd experienced what you've been through I'd need more than a purse full of weapons."

"I've been looking for him today," Liz admitted. "At the diner, at the spa, on the streets. Even here, where he shouldn't be at all. He's dead and I can't stop looking for him."

"You need to be kinder to yourself. If I were telling you this story, that's what you'd say to me."

That was probably true but…

"I would say that but I wouldn't understand how shitty this all is, and how tired you are of being stuck in the past."

Tapping her chin, Celia smiled. "I have some thoughts on this situation. I'm going to talk to Mallory and Dani about them. Stay tuned. This might actually be something that will help."

"I'm all for that. What did you have in mind?"

Celia shook her head. "I won't say yet. I need to talk to them first. They may say that it's a terrible idea."

"I've had several of those lately. Welcome to the club."

"I'm not so sure about that. Things are looking up for you with your new career and now Noah. I think he's just what you've been needing."

Liz couldn't argue that but the real question was… Was she what Noah needed? She had a terrible feeling that the answer was a resounding no.

✦   ✦   ✦

"MAYBE WE SHOULD talk about this later."

Liz and Noah were sitting on the back porch of Dizzy's house. It was late and the barbecue was long over. Mallory, Celia, and Dani were in the living room relaxing after another long day but they would be turning in soon. Tomorrow was the last day before the "big" day and they had a great deal to do – all the last minute details before the wedding including viewing the flower arrangements at the florist, the cake at the bakery, the final meeting with the wedding planner, and of course, the rehearsal and rehearsal dinner. Liz was tired just thinking about all they needed to do.

Note to self. Elope.

"I know it's late," Noah replied with a grimace. "I hate to bug you with all of these details."

Then why are you still doing it?

Uncomfortable. That was the word for what she was feeling. She was uncomfortable with all of his questions.

"This isn't the best time. I'm tired and the girls are ready to go to bed. I should be, too."

Hours ago. Emotions were exhausting, especially fear and anxiety. She felt like she could sleep for a week.

"I just want to make sure that you get what you need, and I'd like to start working on it as soon as possible."

It was the pottery studio Noah wanted to build for her in back of his house. He'd peppered her with questions since they'd arrived home and now, she had a nasty headache, making it difficult to concentrate.

Not to mention be in a good mood. When she was tired, she got cranky.

"I know, but honestly I'm afraid that if I answer your questions right now that I'll tell you wrong. I'm done thinking for the night."

She tried to make light of the situation, pushing back gently at Noah's insistence. He was being incredibly generous and accommodating and she didn't want to seem ungrateful, but...

She didn't want to talk about it right now. Maybe tomorrow. Or the day after. What was the hurry? Why was he pushing this at eleven o'clock at night?

"You're right, it is late. I could always travel with you back to

Denver and take a look at your setup myself."

He'd mentioned that before but she hadn't been sure he was serious.

"Could you leave the ranch?"

"I don't like to do it often, but I could. I have an excellent second-in-command, plus my dad and uncle would love a chance to get their hands dirty. Not sure if my mom and aunt would be all that thrilled, though. They're supposed to be retired."

Liz was of two minds about Noah accompanying her back to Denver. Part of her loved the idea of having him with her, but there was another part of her – a small part – that was beginning to be quite vocal tonight. Speaking louder and louder, drowning out all the other voices. It didn't think that any of this was a good idea.

None of it.

"I could always just take pictures for you."

"That would probably work, although it wouldn't be nearly as much fun."

Could a human being jump out of their skin? Was it possible? Because if it was, she was definitely going to do it. Jump right out of this chair, run around the backyard, and scream at the top of her lungs.

She needed space and time. She needed…to be alone.

"It's late," she blurted. "Can we do this tomorrow?"

I'm in a bad mood and it's only getting worse. Please go home, Noah, before I say something stupid and hurtful.

Too late. She'd already hurt his feelings. She could see it in his eyes.

Dammit.

His arm had been around her shoulders, but now he'd withdrawn it before levering up from the porch swing. Shit, she'd upset him and that's not what she'd set out to do.

"We can do this tomorrow."

Sighing, she rubbed at her pounding temples. "I'm sorry, Noah, but I'm tired. It's been a hell of a day and I'm exhausted. I can barely think straight. I promise I'll be more myself in the morning."

He turned away from her so he was looking out onto Dizzy's backyard. The moon and stars overhead did little to illuminate his features. He could be furious or fine. She had no idea.

"I'm getting the feeling that you don't want me to go to Denver with you."

He wasn't fine, that was for sure. He didn't sound furious either, but the words came out clipped and chilly. He wasn't a happy man, and it was all her fault. Everything was her fault.

"I'm not saying that."

She'd barely had any patience when they'd started this conversation and she was just about at the end of it now.

"I'm getting the feeling that you're pushing me away."

Scraping her hands down her face, she groaned inwardly. There was no getting around this. They were going to argue.

"I am pushing you away. For tonight. I'm exhausted and frankly, in a lousy mood. It's been a shitty couple of days, Noah, and I need to sleep. I've said it once but I'll say it again, I'll be a new person in the morning. Please give me some space tonight."

He didn't want to. She could see it in the tense line of his body and his stubborn chin, illuminated by the porch light.

What was his deal? Why was doing all of this tonight so important?

"I'm not trying to make things more difficult for you." There was hurt in Noah's tone and she'd put it there. He didn't understand and why should he? She barely understood herself. All she knew was that she needed to crawl away and lick at her wounds for a little while. Alone. "I genuinely want to be there for you, Liz."

"I know you do," she replied as patiently as possible. She could see it was in Noah's nature to be protective. She loved that but not right now. "And I'm grateful for that. But I'm asking you to give me some space. I just want to get some sleep."

He stepped forward into the light and now she could see his whole face. It was right there. He wasn't bothering to hide it.

Fear. It was an emotion she knew all too well.

Fuck and hell.

What she didn't know for sure was what he was afraid of.

Was he afraid she wanted far more space than he was comfortable giving?

Was he afraid that she wanted permanent space?

Was he afraid that she'd have Kenneth McGuire sightings when he wasn't here?

Or was he afraid that she would always be this emotional basket case?

He wasn't alone on that last one because she was afraid of it, too.

"Noah, I know you're trying to help and I know that you want me to be okay, but I'm telling you that I need some space tonight. Can you give it to me? Please?"

Her heart plummeted when indecision crossed his handsome features. He was pushing her and she only had one response to that action.

Stepping back. It was the inevitable reaction, all instinct. Her mind and heart might be telling her to stay but that voice in the back of her head was loud and difficult to ignore.

"I can," he said, his head hung in defeat. She'd disappointed him. It was probably the first time of many. "I just wish you could share this with me."

"I've shared more with you than I have with just about any-one else. I can't give you what I don't have. You're asking me to tell you how I feel and I'm trying to tell that I don't know yet. When I do, I'll tell you."

Noah moved toward the back door and then paused, placing his hand on Liz's shoulder. It was strong and warm and oh so tempting. It would be easy to curl up in his arms and pass on her problems to him. Let him worry about it all for awhile, be the strong one. But it wasn't his burden to carry. This baggage belonged to her and she had to deal with it.

"I'll walk you to your car."

Without another word, they walked through the house and out the front door. Noah had parked in the large driveway and they stood next to his driver's door, both of them looking for the right thing to say.

I have to make this right. Make it better.

"I know you just want to help me," Liz said again. "It's just…it seems that you think helping me means solving it all and making it go away. I'm not really sure that's how it works."

Noah was a great guy but he wasn't a superhero. She didn't

expect him to be one, either.

"If you need time and space then I'll give it to you," Noah replied, his voice gruff. He hadn't looked her in the eye in far too long. "I just…"

Want me to be better…fixed. There. I finished that sentence for you.

"I'll call you in the morning."

Should they kiss or hug? Hell, maybe shake hands and slap each other on the back? Liz didn't have a clue as to how she was supposed to act at a moment like this. She had a sudden urge to kick him in the shins for being a stubborn jackass.

I'm not asking for anything that's unreasonable.

He leaned down and brushed his lips over hers once and then climbed into his truck. She stood in that same spot until long after the red taillights disappeared into the darkness, her heart aching in her chest.

Love hurt.

Yes, love. She loved Noah Anderson but she didn't like him much at the moment. He didn't understand that she wasn't a broken clock that just needed a few parts to be good as new. Love could do many wondrous things but it couldn't make her world all better overnight. It had only been a few days and he was already beginning to lose patience.

Was she fooling herself that they could make this work?

Chapter Twenty-Four

"**H**E'S REALLY DEAD."

No beating around the bush. Noah's cousin just laid it out there, quick and to the point. Jason had sent him a text early the next morning and that's why Noah was sitting in his cousin's kitchen drinking coffee and nibbling on a cinnamon roll.

"Okay, you seem very sure."

Jason stood and refilled his coffee cup. "I am sure. I talked to the warden personally. He saw Kenneth McGuire's dead body. In fact, he was there when he died in the infirmary. McGuire didn't even make it to the hospital because his injuries were so serious. He's definitely gone."

Heaving a sigh, Noah had to surrender. "So that's that. Thank you for checking again. I know that I'm a pain in the—"

"Nah, forget it. I see where you're coming from. I would have done the same for Brinley."

"I'm still grateful. I can tell her that he's one hundred per-cent gone and he won't be coming back. I hope that will ease her mind a bit. She was upset last night about thinking she saw him again."

"I would imagine that she would be."

"I wanted to stay with her but she said she needed her space."

Noah was still stinging from that and it must have showed by the look on Jason's face.

Pressing his lips together, Jason rubbed at the back of his neck. "Can I give you some advice? From someone who understands what your girlfriend is going through."

Jason had worked for the DEA and had been taken prisoner by a drug cartel. After he'd escaped, he'd struggled to deal with his trauma for a long time. Being with Brinley had helped, but ultimately, he'd needed professional therapy to move past it.

"I wouldn't mind some advice. In fact, I'll take all the help I can get at this point."

"You can't help Liz."

Wait...what?

The look on Noah's face must have given away his shock at his cousin's statement. "I didn't mean for it to come out like that. What I meant was, the person that has to help Liz is Liz. You can be there for her, you can support her, you can be her biggest cheerleader but when it comes right down to it, she has to do the work. Some of it just takes time and some of it takes a hell of a lot more. But I know you, and I know how you think. You want to solve Liz's problem. You want to take action and fix it, make it all better, but it isn't that simple. You can't do A, B, and C and then she'll be good as new."

"I don't think that," Noah said defensively. "I'm just trying to help her, which apparently was the wrong thing to do last night."

Jason shook his head. "Because you weren't going to be any help. That's why she asked you to leave."

"I told her I could just be there for her," Noah argued. "She said she needed to be alone."

"Then leave her alone," Jason shot back. "You can't fix her issues just be being in the same room with her, and stop questioning that she knows what she needs. After this much time, she knows. The fact is she may never be the person that she was. She may always have some trauma from what she's experienced. Shit, there are nights that I can't sleep a wink or that when I do fall asleep, I have a nightmare. That may happen when I'm old and gray. We're a product of what happens to us. Liz has been through more than many. You have to be okay with who she is *right now*, not who she was or who she might be in the future."

"I am okay with who she is," Noah replied. He sounded defensive because that's how he felt. Was his cousin accusing him of only wanting Liz if she was all better? "I'm fine with it."

Jason quirked an eyebrow. "I just want you to be sure, because the last thing that woman needs is for you to say that you are and then later you aren't. That would set her back and she doesn't deserve that. So you need to be okay with her carrying a gun and checking out the people around her and generally being suspicious wherever she goes, but she can't promise you that she'll stop doing it. Even if she does stop, that doesn't mean it will be forever. She could see, hear, or even read something that triggers those behaviors. And for the love of all that's good and holy, if she needs some time alone, give it to her. Christ, it's not that much to ask."

Noah hadn't heard that many words from Jason in…years.

Maybe never. He'd always been quiet, but since the drug cartel he'd become even more introverted. But always watchful. It was as if Jason was taking in everything and everyone around him.

That fact slapped Noah in the face. Hard.

"Do you still feel that way?"

Already knowing the answer, Noah waited for his cousin to reply.

"I do, although it's different from day to day. I can go months and it's no big deal, then one day…it is."

"It doesn't show much."

Chuckling, Jason grinned. "Because I've learned how to hide it. Some things will never go away completely, though. Brinley understands."

"So this is a warning?"

"Call it a gentle reminder that life isn't as straightforward as we'd like it to be. One of the things that we all love about you, Noah, is that you're so laid back and relaxed. It's a great quality, but you've fallen for a woman who doesn't have that luxury. Every day feels scary and full of peril."

And my being there won't change that. Fuck. What have I done?

Noah understood what Jason was trying to say. What Liz was going through…he couldn't truly get it, but he would need to be patient. There would be good days and bad ones and he'd need to adjust.

To be honest, if it were any other woman but Liz Noah would be gone. Out of there. He'd be giving them the old, "It's not you, it's me." But with Liz? He wanted to be there. He wanted to do the work even if it was tough.

Holy shit, I'm in love.

He hadn't seen it coming but damn, he wasn't unhappy about it at all.

He'd tell her today. Just as soon as he apologized for giving her a hard time last night.

✦　✦　✦

LIZ STOOD NEXT to the bed and stared into her empty suitcase. After a sleepless night, she'd pulled it out from the closet and placed it open on the mattress.

Contemplating. Thinking. About leaving.

She didn't want to go, but there was a vocal part of her deep inside that was screaming for her to run. Far and fast. She was dreaming if she thought her relationship with Noah would work out. She wasn't good for him, and it would only end in heartbreak for them both.

"Does it do tricks?"

Whirling around, Liz saw Dani standing in the doorway. Her friend entered and quietly closed the door behind her as Mallory and Celia were still asleep.

"Is it okay if I join you?"

Liz tried to stand in front of the suitcase but it was a lost cause. Dani had already seen it.

"Of course."

Dani pointed to the luggage. "So…does it?"

"Does what?"

Liz had had zero caffeine yet, so she wasn't as sharp as she would be about an hour from now.

"Do tricks. You were staring at it so long and hard I thought it might jump off of the bed and dance around."

Her cheeks hot, Liz shook her head. "No, it doesn't do any tricks. I was just... reorganizing my clothes."

Nodding, Dani sat on the bed next to the suitcase. "Reorganizing, huh? What are you thinking? Maybe putting your dirty clothes on one side and your clean on the other?"

"That's an option."

"You have many options," Dani said softly. "Be careful how you choose, though. Don't make a decision in the heat of the moment. Think it through to its inevitable conclusion."

They weren't talking about packing suitcases anymore, if they ever had been. This was why Liz was friends with these women. They knew her, better than she knew herself.

With a sad sigh, Liz sat down on the other side of the luggage. "I think that the inevitable conclusion might be ugly and painful."

"That's your fear talking. You're letting it run your life."

I am, but...

"It's stronger than I am."

The admission hurt, like a sharp knife to the gut.

"I seriously doubt that. You're one of the strongest people I know."

Liz laughed even though she wasn't feeling all that funny. "You're lucky that you didn't just burst into flames. That was a huge whopper you just told there."

"Not a lie." Dani smiled and casually crossed her legs. "You are strong. You've had to be. You just never seem to give yourself any credit for it."

"I don't think that I'm strong enough."

"With that attitude, maybe you're not."

"Is this the tough-love portion of the morning?"

Dani was known for her pragmatic approach to life, and she didn't suffer fools gladly.

"It can be if that's what works. So let's talk about it. You pulled out your suitcase because you were thinking about packing your shit and leaving. Tell me...were you planning to talk to us or were we going to get a short and cryptic note about how you don't want to let us or Noah down?"

Her friend had quickly zeroed in on Liz's rationale, although now that the sun was up it didn't seem like such a great idea.

"I would have told you."

"That's nice. Would you have told Noah? Let me guess...nope. If you told him, you'd end up chickening out."

"I love you, Danielle Elise, but sometimes you can be a real bitch."

"I can," she said proudly, her smile widening. "I practice in front of the mirror when no one's around. But I actually don't think I'm being a bitch here this morning. I think that I'm just telling the truth and you're not enjoying that as much as I am. Am I right?"

Liz didn't answer because they both already knew what she was going to say.

"I can see that my advice really isn't wanted so I'll keep it to myself." Dani stood, walked over to the closet and began removing the few outfits that Liz had hanging in it. "So let's get you packed and on the road. You'll probably want to eat breakfast first since you have a long drive."

Hold on...

Liz jumped up and placed her hands over the hangers.

"What are you doing?"

"Helping you pack."

Not quite sure what to say, Liz took the clothes from her friend's arms. "First of all, I don't need any help packing. And second, I haven't made any decisions. I was only thinking about leaving. Is this some sort of bullshit reverse psychology? That stuff never works even on five-year-olds."

"You were just thinking about it?"

Liz looked her friend right in the eye. "Is that a crime?"

"No, but I can't believe you were even thinking about it."

She couldn't? Really?

"Perhaps you haven't been paying attention."

"I've been paying attention. You've had a rough couple of years, but I never, ever thought that you would bail from your best friend's wedding less than thirty-six hours before the ceremony. That's some cold, selfish shit right there. If you think this is in any way okay behavior maybe it's better if you do go."

Liz dropped the clothes on the floor, tears burning the backs of her eyes. "I wasn't...I wasn't really going to leave."

Dani threw up her hands. "Help me understand. You had your suitcase out and you admit that you were thinking about leaving. But you really weren't going to go? I'm confused."

Shame burned in Liz's heart and tears trickled down her red cheeks. "I'm confused, too. I don't know whether I'm coming or going. I don't know if what I'm doing is right or wrong, good or bad. I want to stay here with Noah but then I think that I might be hurting him worse than if I left. He wants me to be all healed, everything sunshine and roses. I want to be better for him but it's not that easy, and frankly I'm tired of all of this bullshit. I just want my life back. And just to be clear, I'm tired of saying that I want my life back. I'm just tired of it all."

Her legs seemed to crumple underneath her and she ended up sitting on the floor in a pile of clothes. Dani knelt on the floor and wrapped her arms around Liz as all the misery of the last two years came spilling out. She was wracked with sobs and Dani simply rocked Liz until there were no more tears. She was worn out and dehydrated.

Falling back against the wall, Liz took several shuddering breaths, her whole body shaking in the aftermath. "Well...that sucked. I thought tears were supposed to be cleansing and make you feel better."

Dani frowned. "That didn't help? I thought a good cry might so I pushed you a little."

"It didn't."

"Sorry."

They both laughed for a moment at the ridiculousness of the situation until Liz remembered why she'd been crying in the first place.

"I wouldn't have left. I was just..." Liz groaned and rubbed at her red and swollen eyes. She must look a real mess. She wasn't a pretty crier. "I wanted to run away and leave it all behind. Stupid, huh? It would just follow me."

"I get it. I really do. We all wish we could wave a wand and make it all disappear but we can't. I hate that you're afraid all of the time."

"Noah wants to make it all better, too."

"Of course, he does, he loves you. That's normal."

"You don't know for sure that he loves me."

"The hell I don't. Trust me, he does."

This was pure Dani. Always so sure of herself.

"I love him," Liz admitted. "I really do."

Dani nodded. "I know you do, hon. You want to save him from having to go through this with you but you're not getting it. He wants to do this."

"He doesn't know what he's getting into."

"That's a possibility," Dani agreed, levering up from the floor and beginning to hang the clothes back in the closet. "But he's a grown ass man, Liz. He's not some naive kid that doesn't know what life is like. Don't infantilize him, because you don't want him to do that to you, either. You're both adults and can make your own decisions. Don't think that you can make his for him."

Cuddling a sweater close to her chest, Liz swallowed down the acid that was burning her throat. She was literally sick to her stomach at the thought that Noah would get tired of her issues.

"I'm scared."

That's what this all came down to. Fear. But this time she wasn't afraid of being a victim. She was terrified of getting her heart broken.

"There are no guarantees," Dani replied. "I wish I could tell you that there were. I will say that no matter what happens with Noah – or any other man in your life – we'll be here to help you through it. You won't be alone…even when you try to push us away. We'll hang in there. You couldn't get rid of us if you tried. We all deserve each other."

Liz wasn't sure she deserved these amazing and wonderful friends but she wasn't about to question it. She'd simply make sure that when they needed her, she was right there by their side.

"I'm going to need your help. I can't do this alone."

Dani smiled and pulled Liz in for a hug. "*No one* could do it all alone. That's the secret of life. Good friends. My mother told me that when I was a kid. I can't believe I've never said it before to you."

Sniffling, Liz scrubbed at her wet cheeks. "What would I do without you three?"

"Luckily we don't have to even wonder. Now let's get these clothes cleaned up, this suitcase put away, and then make some breakfast for Mallory and Celia."

Liz wasn't alone. She never had been actually, but she'd been reminded today. She had friends, and maybe even love…with Noah. Life didn't look all that bleak from this vantage point.

"Let's do it. I'm starved."

"Mallory's getting married tomorrow," Dani sang as she hung up a cotton blouse. "Maybe you'll be next. Noah and Liz sitting in a tree. K-i-s-s-i-n-g. First comes love, second comes marriage…"

Giggling at her friend's antics, Liz snapped the suitcase shut with a loud click. This fucker was going back in the closet and it wouldn't come out until she was ready to go back to Denver. Preferably with Noah.

"One step at a time. Let's worry about the love part first."

Noah, I love you. Do you love me, too?

Chapter Twenty-Five

W HEN LIZ AND the other women arrived at the Anderson ranch, they were amazed to see three huge tents in the backyard that had been erected for the ceremony and reception. There were also several trucks delivering chairs, tables, linens, dishes, silverware, and so on. The Anderson were a wealthy family but even they didn't have enough forks for three hundred plus people.

"It's like the circus except on a whole different level," Mallory breathed. "I mean...I knew that we'd rented three tents but I guess I didn't get just how gigantic they were going to be. We could fit all of Tremont in them."

"That's a good thing because just about all of Tremont is going to be here tomorrow for your wedding," Celia laughed. "My question is where are they all going to park?"

Liz could answer that question. That was one of the items she and Mallory had worked on before the other two arrived in town. "In the south pasture. There will be a mini bus to transport the guests from the parking area to the wedding, and then back again later. We'll have several running so there shouldn't be a wait."

"What if it rains?" Dani asked, her gaze sweeping the area. She had to be imagining giant mudholes all over the backyard. Honestly, Liz had been afraid of that as well, but she'd been assured that it rarely rained this time of year.

"Don't even say that out loud," Mallory groaned. "That would be a nightmare. Luckily the weatherman says that there isn't a cloud in sight until next Thursday at the earliest."

Mallory was nervous and it showed. A lot. A bunch.

She wasn't bordering on basket case but before lunch she'd cried over the flowers and the florist had panicked. It wasn't anything major, just a small miscommunication regarding the centerpieces, easily and quickly rectified, but the usually unflappable Mallory had been crying tears over...daisies.

In fact, she'd been crying off and on all day. When she wasn't crying, she'd suddenly stop what she was doing, her expression horrified, and then she'd panic about an item on their to-do list that she didn't think was done. They'd assure her that she'd taken care of it days ago and then she'd relax again, only to have it happen about an hour later. In between she'd be fine and happy as if it was any other day. It was emotional whiplash, and once more Liz reminded herself that if she ever got married, she'd elope. She didn't want to go through this herself. The problems she had now were bad enough. She didn't need to add any voluntarily.

Liz could only wonder if Carter was exhibiting any nervousness now that the wedding was almost upon them. The big day was tomorrow.

"There's Carter," Mallory said, relief in her tone. The men were exiting the house through the back door and heading toward the tents for the rehearsal. "I hope he's picked up the tuxes from the tailor. They close at two today. I'd better make sure."

When Mallory was out of earshot, Celia quietly cleared her throat. "We need to keep her calm until tomorrow. At the rate she's going, she's going to be hanging from the light fixtures by nightfall."

"It isn't going to be easy," Liz warned. "Mallory has always been prone to nerves. Remember when she had to give that speech in Communications class?"

Dani grimaced at the memory. "She threw up right before. Let's hope that doesn't happen tomorrow."

"Ginger ale," Celia declared. "And comfort foods. It will settle her stomach."

Liz spied Noah coming around the side of the house. She'd ended their evening badly last night and she wanted to apologize. "Excuse me for a minute. I need to talk to Noah."

Dani smiled and nudged her forward. "Take your time."

To her surprise, Noah greeted Liz with a kiss. She'd expected a chillier reception.

"Hey, can we talk? I need to apologize—"

He shook his head. "No, I need to say I'm sorry. I was way out of line last night."

Tilting her head, she couldn't help but giggle. "Are we proficiently adulting again? It feels like it."

Noah's smile widened. "I think we are. Damn, we're mature as hell. I have this strange urge to update my home insurance policy."

This was one of the things that Liz loved so much about Noah. His goofy personality that meshed so well with her own.

She grabbed his hand. "I'd still like to talk to you. Can we...?"

"Absolutely. How about the gazebo?"

Since the last time they'd been there, she'd heard all about this magic gazebo.

"Sounds good. Let me see if Mallory is okay with it. I know that we're here to rehearse."

Mallory didn't mind as the minister was running late, so Noah and Liz slipped away from the others. It was another beautiful day, sunny and warm with just a hint of a breeze. Liz settled onto the wooden bench and snuggled into Noah's side. He was strong and solid, and she allowed herself the luxury of leaning on him for a few minutes.

"I wanted to apologize about last night," she began. "I know that you were frustrated about me wanting to be alone. I don't think that I explained myself very well."

"No, honey, you did fine. It was me that was making the situation more difficult than it needed to be. You were right when you said that I didn't like what you were telling me. I'm sorry about that, and about being a jerk in general about it all. I had a talk with Jason this morning and I think my head is on a bit straighter than it was last night."

That's interesting. And sweet. He sought out another's opinion.

"You talked to your cousin? What did he say?"

"That I had to be okay with where you are now. That I had to understand that getting better isn't going to be a straight line and that some issues might never go away. He reminded me that I'm not a superhero and I can't fix all of this for you, although I wish I could."

"Wow, he's good."

"He's been in a traumatic situation. I thought he was pretty much all better but he set me straight about it."

"So you're okay if I need time to myself?"

"I am, although I admit that it won't be easy."

"I can deal with that."

His smile disappeared. "I was talking to Jason about another topic, actually. I asked him to check on whether it was possible for Kenneth McGuire to still be alive. Any way at all."

Liz had to remind herself to breathe.

"And?"

Her heart pounded so loudly in her ears she wasn't sure she'd even hear his reply.

Noah shook his head. "He's really dead. Jason personally spoke to the warden. He was there when McGuire died. He's really gone."

No doubt. He was dead.

Taking a shaky breath, Liz nodded. "So that's that. It's good to know. Thank you for asking your cousin."

"Are you okay?"

Am I? Yes, I am. I'm good.

"I am. Of course, that means that I'm seeing things which isn't great, but McGuire faking his own death would have been even worse." Liz frowned as a thought occurred to her. "Were you hoping he was alive?"

"I wasn't hoping either way. I just wanted to make sure."

"That's good. So where does that leave us?"

"At a wedding rehearsal. Ready to get Mallory and Carter

married?"

"I was born ready."

Things were looking up. She had good friends, a wonderful man, and wedding cake to look forward to.

✦ ✦ ✦

LIZ HAD RUN inside the main house to use the bathroom after the rehearsal and before they all left for the rehearsal dinner in town, which was being held at a local restaurant that Mallory and Carter had rented out for the evening. She and Noah were going to drive together and she didn't want to keep him waiting too long. Add in the fact that she was starving, and it meant that she put on lipstick at record speed and flew out the backdoor to meet up with everyone at the tents.

She hadn't gone far when she heard the sound of a child crying. It was soft but distinct. There was no mistake. A child was definitely crying somewhere.

Making her way through the maze of delivery trucks, Liz followed the sound, calling out to the child. One of the delivery workers must have brought their young son or daughter with them today and they may have become separated.

"Hello, where are you? Can you tell me where you are? I want to help you."

"But who will help you?"

A pointy object was stuck in Liz's lower back and she froze, holding her breath for what seemed like forever waiting for the person to speak again. The voice was *not* Kenneth McGuire's, however. It was definitely female.

"Now slowly turn around," the voice commanded. "Keep

your hands where I can see them."

Liz raised her arms from her sides and then slowly turned so she was facing the voice.

The voice was a middle-aged woman with salt and pepper hair, holding a cell phone in her left hand and gun in the right, pointed directly at Liz.

It was Kenneth McGuire's mother. But this time she wasn't crying or being sad. She pressed a button on the cell phone and the crying sound stopped.

It had all been a ruse. Liz was caught in a trap.

I am such an idiot.

"Mrs. McGuire," Liz said, taking a shaky breath. She didn't like looking down the barrel of a gun the second time in her life any more than the first.

There was a difference, however, in that Liz was – supposedly – more prepared for this moment than she had been that day two years ago.

We'll see if I really am.

The older woman smiled. "You remember me. You can call me Theresa."

Theresa McGuire. What in the hell was she doing here? Why is she pointing a gun at me?

"You were at the trial every day."

"You certainly made an impression on me too, Elizabeth. You're the reason Kenny went to prison."

Locking her trembling knees, Liz shook her head in denial. "Your son went to prison because he broke the law. That wasn't my fault."

"It was your testimony that locked down the guilty verdict.

Up until then there was reasonable doubt."

This woman was delusional.

"All of his friends pled guilty. I doubt the jury thought that your son was an innocent bystander."

"Innocent is a legal term. My Ken was a good boy."

Strangely, Liz found herself more angry than frightened. Theresa McGuire had a casual relationship with ethics and truth, and was trying to blame her poor parenting on others.

"Your son terrorized a dozen people he'd never met so he could steal money. That doesn't sound good to me."

Theresa raised her arm higher so the gun was pointed directly at Liz's heart. "Huge corporations make profits off the sweat of the little man. They deserve to be robbed."

"Does the little man deserve to have a gun pointed at him?" Liz demanded as sweat trickled down her back from where it had pooled at the back of her neck. She was nervous but she was angry at the same time. "Your son threatened to kill us one by one. We all thought we were going to die."

The woman shrugged carelessly. "Everyone dies. Kenny died and it's all your fault."

"My fault? How is it my fault?"

"If he hadn't been in prison, he wouldn't have gotten into that fight. He'd be alive except for you. That day when you were on the stand, you made him sound like a monster."

Liz wanted to tell this woman that her son was a monster, but clearly she wouldn't believe it. She'd rationalized her son's behavior in a truly bizarre manner.

"I wasn't the only witness."

"You're right, and they'll all get what's coming to them, too.

Dillon and I will make sure of it. For Kenny."

"Dillon?"

"My other son. He's here with me. In fact, we're going to him."

There was another McGuire? Did he look like Kenneth?

Holy shit, I may not have been seeing things.

Relief flooded Liz's body and she had to force herself to focus on the real problem at hand.

A gun pointed at her.

It was great that she probably wasn't hallucinating but she still had a huge issue right here and now. Getting out of the situation alive.

"You have another son?"

"Kenny's older brother. You'll meet him in a minute. We'll all get in his truck and take a little drive."

And then you'll kill me. I think I'll pass on that.

Stall, Liz. Stall. Eventually Noah will come looking for me. Or someone will walk by. There are dozens of people around here.

"How did you even know I was here in Tremont?"

"That was easy. You were tagged in a photo on social media having dinner with your friends. The minute I saw it, Dillon and I drove down here that night. We've been following you and waiting for just the right moment. This wedding was the perfect opportunity. Chaos. People coming and going. It was so easy to blend in as waiters or delivery people. The people of this town are amazingly stupid and trusting. We just walked up and stole a uniform. No one asked us any questions."

The only photo Liz knew about was the one that had been taken that night at the roadhouse. She hadn't given it a second

"I've been seeing your son around town. He looks a lot like Kenneth."

"He does. Both of them favor my husband." Theresa jerked the gun to the right. "Now it's time to go. Turn around slowly and start walking."

That couldn't happen. After the robbery, Liz had taken self-defense classes for awhile and one of the first rules she'd learned was to never let an attacker take her anywhere. Don't get in the car, don't leave the location. Invariably, the perpetrator would take the victim somewhere remote where the screams wouldn't be heard.

I won't be a victim again. Not this time.

Liz's handgun was in her purse, but it was currently zipped closed and hanging on her right shoulder. If she tried to reach into it, Theresa would probably panic and shoot.

I may have to scream and fight my way out of this.

Taking on Theresa probably wouldn't be that bad. She was an older woman although she appeared to be in decent shape. But Liz definitely couldn't take on Dillon, the son. She'd have to make her move soon, then.

If I just start screaming will she shoot?

The ranch was crawling with people. If Liz started screaming someone was sure to come running but would it be too late? Did Theresa care about getting caught? That was the problem when a person had nothing to lose…logic didn't mean much to them. The sanctity of life meant even less.

And Liz had a hell of a lot to live for. Her friends, family, her new business…and Noah, of course. They'd just found each

240

other and she wasn't going to let her past get in the way of the future that she could have with the man she loved.

Yes, loved.

The weight of Liz's purse hung heavily on her shoulder. Heavy, but useless. The gun was zipped up inside. This is what Mallory, Dani, and Celia had been talking about. The "illusion" of safety. She'd felt safer because she'd been carrying a gun but now that the situation arose to use it…she couldn't get to it.

Wait…the handbag was heavy. It weighed a ton. Mallory had compared it to an anvil at one point.

An anvil in the face could do some serious damage. If, and that was a big if, Liz could manage to swing it around and hit Theresa with it. That would give her a chance to scream and run. All she needed was an opening to get away…

"Move," Theresa commanded again, poking the gun in Liz's back. "We don't have all day."

No, we don't. Now is the time.

Hopefully, Theresa would stay exactly where she was – arms' length from Liz. That was the ideal distance as that was about how long the purse straps were as well.

Taking one tiny step forward, Liz slowly lowered her right shoulder so that the heavy purse slid down her arm and onto the ground with a thud. Theresa growled in annoyance but she didn't move, waving the gun at the handbag.

"Just leave it. Let's go."

That's something I cannot do.

It took effort but somehow Liz managed to keep her voice normal, despite the blood roaring in her ears. She was shocked that Theresa couldn't hear her heart pounding against her ribs like a marching band. "If I leave it and someone finds it, they'll know something has happened to me. They'll immediately be suspicious."

"Fine," Theresa snapped. "Just get it. We need to get moving. Dillon is waiting for us."

He's going to have to wait a lot longer.

Liz bent forward, grasping the strap of the purse close to the bottom with both hands to get the most control. She only had one shot at this. It would either work or be a disaster. There wasn't much in between.

Inhaling sharply, Liz braced herself for the roundhouse swing of a lifetime.

I won't be a victim again.

Chapter Twenty-Six

THE REHEARSAL HAD gone off without a hitch. This wasn't the first time they'd all walked down an aisle in step to the wedding march music, so it was basically just figuring out who was going to stand where and how not to step in front of someone or on the bride's train.

Noah and Liz had walked back down the aisle after the pretend ceremony arm in arm. He'd been standing next to Carter and his other brothers when she'd walked up that same aisle, holding a rose and smiling, looking far more beautiful than anyone should have a right to. She'd been looking at *him* the entire time, their gazes locked with every step.

He couldn't help but think about her wearing a white dress and veil at their own wedding. Yep, he had it that bad. He was already thinking about the future. More specifically...his future with Liz. They'd been through so much and now they had their second chance.

"You walked down the aisle like a pro," Noah said to Liz when the rehearsal was over. "How many times have you done this before?"

Liz groaned and rolled her eyes. "Too many times. Every

time I'm in a wedding I swear that it's going to be the last, but when Mallory asked I couldn't say no, of course."

"Thank goodness you said yes. If you hadn't…"

"I still would have come to the wedding," Liz pointed out. "I still would have seen you and you would have seen me."

The outcome would have been the same. It was fate, after all.

"Are you going to drive into town with me?" Noah asked. Mallory and Carter had rented out a local eatery for the rehearsal dinner tonight. It was a small affair with just the wedding party.

"I can but I really need to freshen up first, if you don't mind waiting five minutes."

"Take as long as you need. I'll wait right here with the guys."

Liz hurried toward the main house and Noah settled into a rented folding chair in the tent. Easton sat down beside him, holding out a can of soda which Noah accepted gratefully. He was parched and it wasn't a surprise that it was his twin who had noticed. They had a sort of thing where they could tell how the other one was feeling. Once Noah had stopped at the store and bought cold medicine because he was convinced that Easton was sick. When he arrived at his brother's house it turned out he was right.

"Thanks, I was damn thirsty. Where's Dizzy?"

"In the house. Mom has something she wants to show Dizzy. Don't ask me what it is because it's some sort of big secret. Maybe it's my birthday present."

"Our birthday is two months away."

"Then I have no idea what Mom is showing her. Dizzy won't tell me, and you know how she is when she's keeping a secret. Where's Liz?"

"She's in the house, too. She won't be long."

Easton glanced over his shoulder at the house in the distance. "Dizzy and I are really happy for you and Liz. She seems like a nice woman."

"Thanks, she's wonderful."

"Carter mentioned that you're going to build a pottery studio for her."

"I am and you're welcome to come help. Get your hands dirty a little."

Laughing, Easton took a long drink from his soda. "We might be twins but we stopped dressing alike and doing everything together when we were kids."

"That's the truth. There was no way we were going to grow up and do the same things—"

Noah broke off, his attention captured by a man strolling toward the area where all the delivery trucks were parked.

Kenneth McGuire? It sure as hell looked like the photo that Jason had sent him along with the other information about the bank robbery. Sure, it was from a distance so he might be wrong, but...

Wait a goddamn second. Noah wasn't the person traumatized by being held hostage in a bank robbery. He shouldn't be seeing dead men. That could only mean one thing – Liz wasn't seeing things. But Jason had sworn up and down that McGuire was dead.

"Are you okay? You look like you've seen a ghost."

Easton's query pulled Noah from his thoughts. His brother was looking at him, a worried expression on his face.

The same face that Noah looked at in the mirror in the

morning.

Fuck.

Jason had said that McGuire had a criminal sibling.

Brothers.

His heart racing, Noah sprang to his feet. If Kenneth McGuire's brother was in Tremont that didn't bode well for Liz's safety. He needed to find the son of a bitch right the hell now. Without a backward glance at his brother, Noah sprinted after the doppelgänger, his boots pounding the uneven ground and his lungs straining to suck in oxygen.

For a moment, he thought that the man had managed to slip away into the labyrinth of trucks but then he turned right and saw him, walking leisurely without a care in the world about ten feet away. Noah was about to change that. With a roar, he tackled the man to the ground and pushed him to his back while Noah straddled him, holding him down. The other guy fought back but Noah didn't have the patience for it. He sunk his fist into the man's gut and the fight went out of him.

And he did look just like Kenneth McGuire, although up close Noah could see the differences. This man was slightly older with more lines around his eyes and mouth. His hair was the same color but clipped shorter than the photograph.

"Why have you been following Liz around? What are you doing here?"

The man tried to look confused and shook his head. "Who's Liz? I'm here to deliver tables and chairs for the wedding tomorrow."

"Bullshit," Noah snarled, keeping a tight hold on the man's shirt. "Why have you been following her around? What do you want? I know that you're Kenneth McGuire's brother, so talk."

At the mention of his brother's name, the man stopped struggling and smiled. "Then I don't need to answer your questions. You know why we're here."

Noah wanted to beat this man's head into the ground. Repeatedly.

He wasn't going to do that, however. But that didn't mean he couldn't tighten his grip on the asshole's shirt and scare him a little. Noah leaned down and invaded the guy's personal space, giving him a shake.

"I asked—"

Hold on a moment. We? We?

"You said *we*. Who else is here?" Noah growled, his patience at an end.

"Mom," the asshole replied promptly with a shit-eating grin. "I'm guessing she's already got your pretty girlfriend."

His mother? The woman that Liz had described as crying every day of the trial?

And she's hunting the woman I love?

Before Noah could respond a shot rang out and the man's smile widened. "Looks like it's too late."

If it was…there wasn't a safe place for this dick and his mother. Noah would make them wish they'd never been born.

NOAH HAD NEVER been so scared in his entire life. Not when he'd been the first of his brothers to go off to college. Not when his girlfriend thought – erroneously – that she was pregnant. Not when Jason was taken prisoner by a drug cartel. Not even when his dad had had a "heart incident" about a year ago.

None of that had prepared him for the sheer terror of losing Liz so soon after he'd found her again. This was supposed to be their second chance and that gunfire might have taken it all away.

Sweat poured off of him and his heart thundered in chest, blocking out everything around him. There was only Liz. No wedding. No family and friends. Just the frantic determination to find her and keep anyone from hurting her. He prayed he wasn't too late. He rounded the back corner of a truck and stopped in his tracks, dragging air into his aching lungs.

Liz. Very much alive.

And a woman, who must have been McGuire's mother, lying on the ground and moaning in pain.

Two steps and he was standing next to Liz and pulling her into his arms. He needed to feel her, and know that was alive and well. He ran his hands over her arms and down her legs, looking for any sign of injury. He'd breathe again when he was sure that she was okay.

"We heard a gun go off. Are you hurt? Do you need a doctor?"

"I'm fine. I'm okay. The gun went off but it fired into the air, I think."

She didn't sound fine or okay. She sounded like she was going to cry, her voice choked and thick. He cupped her chin so she had to look up at him and he could see that her eyes were bright with unshed tears.

"You're hurt," he said. "We'll go to the hosp–"

"I'm not hurt." This time she spoke more firmly, placing her hand over his. "I swear, I'm okay. I'm just...overwhelmed."

The clearing of a throat had Noah turning around to see Easton, Carter, Shane, Jason, and West all standing there. Jason, with West on his heels, nodded to Liz and gave her an encouraging smile before heading straight for McGuire's mother on the ground, hauling the complaining woman to her feet. She kept saying she needed a doctor. She'd see the local sheriff first.

Easton shrugged. "You ran. So I did, too. If I see my twin running as if a crazed killer clown with a butcher knife is chasing him, you bet your ass I'm going to follow."

Noah looked at his other brothers. "What's your story?"

A smile played on Carter's lips. "It's my fucking wedding, asshole. If anyone is going to get in a fight, get dirty, or catch a bad guy I'm going to be in on it."

"That was pretty much my thinking as well," Shane replied with a straight face. "We heard the gunshot, too. It's good to see that you're okay, Liz."

She was okay. Noah was beginning to finally believe it, and his heart rate was going back to normal. The gray hairs he'd sprouted in the last five minutes? Those were going to be permanent.

"What did happen here?"

Rubbing at her temples, Liz took a deep breath before answering. "I heard a child crying so I walked around looking for them. I figured one of the delivery people had brought their kid and they'd been separated."

Shane nodded. "Logical assumption."

"Then I felt something sticking in my back. It was Theresa McGuire, Kenneth McGuire's mom, and she's holding a gun.

She showed me a cell phone that had a recording of the crying child, and then tells me that we're going to meet her son Dillon and go for a drive. Needless to say, I didn't like the sound of that. So I pretended to drop my purse and then I picked it up and hit her with it as hard as could." Her eyes went wide, and she went to move past Noah. "Shit, we have to find him. He could—"

"We've got him, honey," Noah said softly. "I saw him and well…fuck, it's a long story but I punched him."

Liz looked up at him in amazement. "You punched him?"

"I did."

Her surprise turned to happiness. "Good. He deserved it. Where is he now?"

Shit, where was he?

"Our cousins are taking care of him," Carter answered. "And the sheriff is on his way."

Noah reached down and picked up Liz's handbag that was sitting on the ground. Damn thing weighed a ton, of course. She had an arsenal in it.

"I guess that gun for personal protection came in handy, after all."

Her smile fell. "They were following me. That's what she said. I wasn't seeing things. They were following me around just waiting for the right moment."

There were sirens in the distance. The cavalry had arrived but Liz hadn't needed them.

"You're weren't a victim again. You did what you said you were going to do."

"I thought this would feel different. I thought I would

feel…"

"Triumphant?"

"Maybe," she nodded, snuggling close, her cheek on his chest. "Or maybe I thought it would solve all my problems. That everything would go back to the way it was before the bank robbery."

"I don't think it works that way." Noah threw a quick glance over his shoulder at his family, giving them a scowl that told them to scatter. He had things to say to this woman and he didn't want them to listen in. Jason and West had already vacated the area with the groggy but belligerent Mrs. McGuire. "When I heard the gunshot…fuck, Liz…I thought I might have lost you, and if that had happened…I don't know what I would do. You've become everything to me. I guess what I'm trying to say it that I love you. I love you so much."

Those tears that Liz had been holding back streamed down her cheeks. "I love you, too. So very much. I can't believe I've found you again, and I can't believe that you love me."

Cupping her damp cheeks in his hands, Noah pressed a soft kiss to her lips. Gazing into her amber-colored eyes, his heart squeezed painfully in his chest. This was love. The real thing and he'd waited so damn long to find it.

She'd been worth waiting for.

"Believe it. The universe has spoken. You're stuck with me."

"I can live with that."

He'd be happy to as well.

Chapter Twenty-Seven

L IZ KEPT HER gaze locked on Noah as she walked slowly up the aisle. He looked incredibly handsome in his tuxedo, his hair tamed, and his jaw freshly shaved. He was standing with his brothers, all in a row, every one of them happy and smiling. But Noah's smile…it was just for her.

It wouldn't be half bad to see that smile every day for the rest of her life. She might be jumping the gun but she knew that she loved Noah Anderson. He loved her, too. Now it was up to them to make it work. It wouldn't be easy, of course. She still had some issues to work on, but Noah seemed to understand that while he could be there for her and help, he couldn't completely solve the problems that had plagued her since the bank robbery. However, yesterday had gone a long way to push her over a big hurdle.

She'd always said she wouldn't be a victim again and she'd kept that promise. She'd stood up to the McGuires and used the skills she'd learned to survive. She wasn't sure what had happened inside of herself but now she wasn't as scared as before. Her worst nightmare had come true and she'd faced her demons. Fear wasn't hanging over her head anymore.

Liz was…better…stronger…more confident. She'd never be able to go back to who she had been before but she could be someone different, someone not afraid of every dark corner or noise. It wasn't all resolved and it might never be, to be honest. She could take steps backward in the future but now she was sure she could take the steps forward as well. She wouldn't be a burden to Noah, she could be his partner.

The rest of the wedding went off without a hitch, just as they'd all rehearsed. Food was consumed, toasts made, and the multi-tiered wedding cake cut. Mallory was dancing cheek to cheek with Carter along with most of the other couples. The lights in the tent were low and the atmosphere one of pure romance.

"Look at them," Dani sighed as the three women stood on the edge of the dance floor watching the newlyweds. "They're so much in love."

Celia, who was the softie of the group, sniffled into a tissue. "It sort of renews your faith in humanity seeing them look at each other like that, doesn't it?"

"It certainly does," Liz agreed. "In fact, I think this entire trip to Tremont has restored my faith."

"Not many people go to a wedding and leave with the love of their life," Dani declared with a grin. "Not to mention that you helped capture a couple of criminals. Speaking of, way to go."

Liz's cheeks warmed. "You said that last night."

"We meant it," Celia laughed. "And we mean it now. You're one badass chick. Next time I'm in a dark alley, I want you by my side."

"I had a little help from Noah and everyone else."

"I have a feeling you would have been fine on your own," Dani said with a knowing wink. "Those two McGuires never stood a chance. You're like…Dirty Harriet. Or Liz Claude Van Damme."

"I don't think I qualify but thanks for the ego boost. I didn't take on a dozen ninjas or anything." Liz's throat grew tight. "I couldn't have survived this week without all three of you. You're my best friends and I can't imagine my world without you."

Dani threw her arm around Liz's shoulders. "Aww, honey, we feel the same. We're not just friends. We're family and you know you can't get away from family."

"You'll never get away from us," Celia said. "Ever. We were meant to meet that first day at school. It was fate. Or the universe. Whatever it was, it sure wasn't finished with you. Looks like your man wants to dance."

It did look like that. Noah was standing a few feet away, beckoning her to come join him. He'd shed his tuxedo jacket earlier along with the vest and tie. He wasn't the type to dress up, and frankly, he was far too sexy in his white shirt with a few buttons undone, his hair slightly askew.

Dani gave her a nudge. "Go on, girl. Go get 'em."

Liz didn't need any more urging. She hurried into his arms, letting Noah swing her around before pulling her close. Every inch of her was pressed close to his warm body and she buried her nose into his open shirt and breathed deeply, letting his yummy scent surround her. When she was in his arms like this, it was as if they were the only two people left in the world.

They swayed to the music for awhile, oblivious to anyone around them until he eventually pulled away and gently began leading her toward the door. The exited the tent and walked the short distance to the gazebo.

"Look at the stars," Noah whispered in her ear as she leaned back against him. "We didn't have stars like this that night in Chicago."

"No, but we had something else."

Liz kept her voice low as well, although there wasn't anyone around to hear them. It just made it seem more intimate and special.

"We did? What's that?"

"Magic, and it was so powerful it brought us back together again."

His lips were right next to her ear, his breath warm on her cheek. "If I ask you to marry me sometime in the future, will you say yes? I know that it's too early now but I want you to know what I'm hoping for."

It was too soon. Right? Funny, it didn't feel too quick.

They'd come too far together for her to play coy.

"I'll say yes."

His arms tightened around her and he turned her so they were looking into each other's eyes. "I love you. As you are. You don't have to do or be anything different. In my eyes, you're perfect."

She'd already cried during the ceremony but he had her doing it again. A few fat tears slid down her cheeks but she paid them no mind. She had a feeling this wouldn't be the last time this man had her crying tears of joy.

"I love you too, Noah Anderson. From the moment I met you, you were in my heart."

It was fate that brought them together the first and second time, but it was love that would keep them together now and into the future.

✦   ✦   ✦

One year later...

DIZZY'S MOTHER TAMI was dancing around the hospital room playing a tambourine, while her husband Louis slapped at a set of bongos. Easton sat next to Dizzy on the bed and held her hand through each contraction and the rest of them held lit candles and cringed. Her contractions were getting stronger and more painful but Liz and everyone else were aware that Dizzy wanted to do this without an epidural. She'd been talking about it since she'd announced her pregnancy.

She'd wanted to have a home birth but with carrying twins, her doctor had strongly urged her to deliver her babies in a hospital in case anything went south. Dizzy, of course, had agreed but had wanted the atmosphere to be as homelike as possible with family around her, laughing, making jokes, singing, and the women telling their own birth stories.

And that's the way it had gone for the first twenty hours or so but now at hour thirty things were beginning to get dicey...

"You're doing great, honey," Easton encouraged, mopping at Dizzy's damp forehead. "I'm so proud of you."

Curling her lip in disgust, Dizzy only turned away, this time to speak to her father.

"Louis, for the love of the Goddess, stop that infernal racket," she yelled, her cheeks going even redder than they already were. "And Tami, you too. I agreed to the candles but I didn't agree to this."

Tami paused, her expression puzzled. "You said that music would be nice while you were in labor."

"Music, yes," Dizzy snapped. "That's not music. That's a one-way ticket to a migraine. Everyone just shut up. No one talks. Not one word. Got it?"

Dizzy's pointed stare ran around the room and everyone one of them did as she asked, not wanting to upset her any more than she already was. Noah grabbed Liz's hand and even took a step closer to the door. Shane, his wife Arden, Carter and Mallory, and both sets of parents instantly fell silent.

"Sweetheart," Easton said in his most soothing tone. "How about some ice chips? That might make you feel better."

Easton held up a paper cup filled with ice chips and tried to smile encouragingly but Dizzy didn't appear to appreciate his helpfulness. Her eyes went round and she grabbed at the front of Easton's button down shirt.

"I don't want ice chips," she snarled. "I need–"

That's when another contraction started, right on top of the last one with hardly any respite for Dizzy. Tami was instantly at her daughter's side, hopping from one foot to the other.

"That's it, let it take you. Let it push the babies into our world. If it gets too much, just scream. Scream, Dizzy, scream. You'll feel better. That's what I did when I was having you."

Louis opened his mouth to add something to his wife's memories of childbirth but he didn't get a chance to get anything out. Instead, Dizzy opened her mouth as well and let out a scream that sounded like something out of horror movie and she was being chased by a crazed axe murderer. Liz had to wonder if she might now be bleeding from her ears. Noah's hand tightened painfully on Liz's and he'd turned a peculiar shade of white.

Do I need to get him out of here?

"That's it," Tami said, her smile beaming. She clapped her hands together as if applauding a soprano at the Met. "Keep doing that. It will help with the pain."

Needing no other prodding, Dizzy screamed again, the sound echoing off the walls and tile floors. Liz was sure they could hear her down the hall and in the parking garage.

Still having a grip on Easton's shirt, Dizzy yanked him closer. "Find a doctor. Any doctor. Get me something for this pain."

"Now, Dizzy, you said you wanted to do this naturally," Tami began but snapped her mouth shut when her daughter gave her the look of death.

Dizzy tried to sit up in the bed but fell back against the pillows, drained of energy. "Naturally? Are you kidding? I'm about to push two human beings out of me, Tami. You only did one. You lied to me. You said it didn't hurt that bad. *You lied.* I need something and I want it now. I don't care what I said before."

Easton hit the door running. Presumably to find a doctor, nurse, anesthesiologist, or even someone who played a doctor on television but had no real medical training. Another contraction hit Dizzy, and her mother and Easton's mom Kathy each held one of her hands as she screamed. They kept talking about how beautiful her babies were going to be and how well she was doing. They were all holding their collective breath when Easton returned with two doctors who immediately shooed them out of the room so they could give Dizzy an epidural.

Not one person argued as they were pushed into the hallway and waiting room. The last few hours had been tense, to say the least, and Liz was exhausted and she hadn't been the one birthing two new Andersons.

Noah sagged against the wall. "Whew, that was intense. Poor Dizzy is having a hell of time in there."

"Easton, too," Liz replied. "I feel for them both. This baby stuff isn't like in the movies."

Flicking a glance over his shoulder, Noah sneakily laid a hand on Liz's tummy, and she placed her own on top. He was doing this more and more lately and she loved it. "This didn't scare you? Because it scared the shit out of me. I don't want you in any pain when you go into labor."

Liz was eight weeks pregnant as of yesterday. They hadn't told anyone yet because they didn't want to steal Dizzy and Easton's thunder, plus they weren't out of the first trimester.

They also hadn't mentioned that they'd snuck off to Las Vegas a few weekends ago and quietly married in a lovely little chapel. Only the two of them, and just the way they'd wanted it. They were planning on telling their entire families but it was kind of fun to have secrets just for a few weeks.

"There's scared and then there's *scared*," Liz laughed. "All that meditation that Dizzy has had me doing paid off. I'm almost as laid back and mellow as you are."

"I don't know how Easton is doing this. I couldn't imagine seeing you in that much pain and being helpless to do anything about it."

Liz gazed up into her worried husband's eyes. They were dark with emotion but she could see the love there as clearly as if he'd screamed it as loud as Dizzy had. There had been ups and down in the last year – and there would be in the future – but they'd been determined from the very beginning that they were going to work as a team when they came to obstacles. So far, they'd been *adulting* like experts.

"You'll be fine," Liz assured him, lifting a hand to cup his stubbled jaw. He was so handsome. All the Anderson men were, but with Noah it was more than just classical good looks. It was…integrity. Love. Care. Compassion. Strength. He was more than she'd ever hoped for and he was all hers. "We'll do it together."

The world might be a scary place but with Noah by her side, she could face it all.

It was only two hours later when Easton burst out of the room to tell gathered family that Dizzy had just given birth to their two sons – Camden Alexander and Nathan Christopher – both healthy. Mother doing fine. Easton, however, looked a trifle worse for wear but he was also wearing the most breathtakingly happy smile Liz had ever seen.

"They're a family," she whispered, cuddling closer to Noah. "We're a family, too."

Noah nodded toward the assembled Andersons – the others would soon be there to greet the latest arrivals into the clan. "We were always a family. No one circles the wagons more tightly than the Andersons. We'll love and protect you forever."

Forever with this man? She'd take it. The universe had spoken.

Thank you for reading! I hope you enjoyed Dancing With Danger. There will be more stories in the Cowboy Justice Association/Danger Incorporated world. Coming soon.

About The Author

Olivia Jaymes is a wife, mother, lover of sexy romance and cozy mysteries, and caffeine addict. She lives with her husband, son, and two spoiled dogs in central Florida and spends her days typing on her computer with a canine on her lap.

She is currently working on a new cozy mystery series – *A Ravenmist Whodunit* – in addition to her other ongoing romance series.

Visit Olivia Jaymes at

www.OliviaJaymes.com